PROPHETS TANGO

se OUT OF STEP

DEBORAH LACATIVA

PROPHETS TANGO

by Deborah Lacativa

A novel serialized in three parts:
Season One—Out of Step
Season Two—Dancing in the Dark
Season Three—The Light Fantastic

www.lacativa.com

ISBN: 978-1-7351434-3-9

Cover by Bookfly Design

Interior by Grace Wynter

PROPHETS TANGO

SEASON ONE: OUT OF STEP

PROLOGUE

For the lucky living, the night was ripe. 1974 was the Year of the Tiger—Nixon was running scared, Ted Bundy was just getting started, and the tallest buildings in the world had opened down on Wall Street. Everyone who was underage in Connecticut was welcome in New York. All the doors of the Stateline bar were open wide to the night and the place was packed.

The smoke-laden air inside the joint pulsed out into the heat and humidity of the fecund darkness and flowed back inside with a heavy tinge of marijuana. There was a furtive commotion in a dark corner of the parking lot. Fighting or fucking, it didn't matter. April was in a hot hurry to be July.

The amplified sounds of a live rock band complete with horns hushed all the night creatures around the ramshackle country bar for a quarter mile in every direction. The music held sway over all, from those in worn, holey denim to the spandex and polyester crowd up from the city. The band— consummate crowd-pleasers—smoothly moved from rock to disco, to funk and blues with occasional stops at country and doo-wop along the way, and none could resist the urge to move to the beat.

Tonight, the revelers included a woman with no heart, a man with no soul, and a pair of mismatched, hapless spirits on assignment.

PERCHED on a stool at the bar, Anna worked at drinking herself into a state of safety, insulating herself from the rioting mental scatter of the other patrons. While fishing for money in the depths of her purse, she'd found a dusty, travel-worn pill. Small, greenish, the embossed markings illegible, she'd shrugged and washed it down with the last swallow of her second tequila sunrise. *Que será, será.*

A syrupy warmth flooded her body, the noise and jagged energy of the crowd receded, and she took a long, deep breath that lifted her taller in her seat, her guarded cynicism spinning away like a bad dream. Thirsty with the sudden heat, she scanned the top-shelf liquor.

Wary of the change in her demeanor, the bartender said, "Honey, if you're gonna be sick, take it outside."

Anna smiled in slow motion, licked her lips, and focused on him with devilish intensity. "Thanks for the concern, Sal, but I've never felt better." She held her glass up like Lady Liberty's torch. "Another one of your masterpieces will crown my evening if you don't mind. Double the cherries and," she spread her last ten across the sticky bar top, "keep the change."

Gina stood beside Anna with her back to the bar, watching the crowd of dancers drifting back to their tables as the band vamped. She shouted over her shoulder to the bartender. "Go ahead. Blitz her. Looks like I'm driving tonight, anyway."

. . .

AT A CROWDED TABLE on the far side of the room, Jack was growing bored with the rowdy conversation and laughter. He tilted his chair back on its hind legs, idly testing to see if, after hours of partying, he could still duel with gravity and win.

The trick, he'd learned from a circus tightrope walker, was to relax from the center of your being outward. Quiet your mind, and your body would find the way. For a string of enchanted seconds, Jack floated, arms spread at the perfect point of balance. He was ready to flap his wings and fly when the band started back up, drums and guitars grabbing his pulse, his focus. His chair wobbled and one of the girls shrieked, "Jack! You're gonna break your ass!"

Over the music, he heard the intimate whisper and felt the invisible caress that had lately been pulling him back from the edge, back to life.

WHEN SHE WAS ALIVE, Hope had been a lady of the night. Tall and elegant, she was beautiful, self-educated, and wise beyond the narrow scope of her world in New Orleans. She'd lived after the Great War, but before the Depression brought the country to its knees. Born to the trade, she thought well of herself and her sisterhood. She never questioned why her spirit lingered after her body had failed. She was on a mission.

Samuel Archer Fortune had been an apprentice woodsman from western Massachusetts. He was only seventeen when he'd been killed wondering *Why?* when everyone else was yelling: "Run!" It happened his last day felling trees for the railroad in New York State after which he'd intended on enlisting with the

Union Army. His mother was grateful to know he'd been buried decently where he'd died. In time, she might rebury him in the family plot with the rest of the ancestors. Many of the local boys who'd gone to the fight would never come home, bodies left where they fell, lost in the maw of war forever.

Death had taken Hope and Sam by surprise when both were young and still optimistic. The two spirits stood in the bar's open side door, shoulder-to-shoulder, oblivious of the patrons who, equally unaware, passed through them with the drifts of smoke. Although Hope stood a head taller, Sam was a formidable presence, dense with unused physical strength.

So far, Hope had no way of knowing if Jack—Jackson Jude Bell, ladies' man, hooligan, drug dealer, and holy assassin—would be her last connection with the living, or not. What *was* clear to her was, as spirits go, Sam was as green as new grass.

"Are you telling me she's your first assignment?"

"I don't even know what you mean by that," Sam replied.

"Her," She pointed her sharp chin towards the bar. "Over on the end stool. She with the big caboose."

Sam studied Anna like he was appraising a heifer at an auction. She shimmered in the light of his gaze.

"I have an affinity for her that I don't understand," he said wistfully. Then he clutched at his hair and moaned, "Is this what being dead is all about? Am I a peeping ghost? What happened to my eternal rest?"

"Oh, child." Hope looked beseechingly at the ceiling, "What icehouse have they kept you in?" She closed her eyes and tried to come up with the most basic explanation for him. "Yes, this is your job now. Can you read?"

"Of course," he said, folding his muscular arms across

his chest. He was dressed in heavy brogans, wool trousers, and a rumpled brown linen shirt. His thick, blond hair looked goat-chewed rather than barbered. "Just because I'm a provincial don't make me illiterate."

Hope stifled a smirk. "Easy, easy brother. I was just thinking about something I read on a sign somewhere, 'Protect and Serve' it said. Well, that's what we're here for, but I'll warn you, it's no easy job when they pay so little attention. Looks to me like your girl is as dumb as a post as far as you're concerned." She thought about how long it had taken her to get Jack's attention, and how he still ignored her half the time.

Sam squinted across the room to see Anna raise her empty glass to the bartender. He scowled.

"She's inebriated. They all are! These times are steeped in sin. This must be my punishment," he said, hanging his shaggy head.

Hope almost felt sorry for him. "You'll have to get over passing judgment—not your place, you know."

"Can they even hear us?"

"Sometimes, but not with their ears. We have to open their eyes, their hearts. Make them see what holds weight. I'm Hope, by the way. Looks like I'll be showing you the ropes." She heaved a sigh. A woman's work is truly never done.

Sam looked Hope up and down. Everything about her, her cropped hair, the flimsy dress that exposed her arms and legs, her world-weariness, shouted "sinner." As inexperienced as he was, he knew a harlot when he saw one. "And just how is it you know so much, pray tell?"

Hope looked at him like he'd grown a third eye. "God, but you're a rube. Where did you say you were from?"

"Danford, Massachusetts," he replied as if it was somewhere that mattered.

"Never heard of it." She sniffed and tossed her shawl higher on her shoulder. "Never you mind about my business. Men and boys like you paid big money for my time." It dawned on her that Sam had no idea what she was talking about. He'd surely been a virgin when that widow-maker stove in his head, likely only rarely acquainted with his right hand, sin that it was and all. His blue eyes, wide in his snub-nosed, ruddy face, were tracking every pretty girl in sight, but the tracks all led back to Anna.

Hope watched him out of the corner of her eye. *Is he lying to me or is he really in the dark about her?* She only had bits and pieces of Anna's story. Had she caught Sam in a lie or the true bliss of ignorance?

"It was you with her in Boston, am I right? And the other time outside that juke joint?"

Sam blushed and looked down at his feet, but his gaze shifted back to Anna with a fierceness that surprised Hope.

"I was glad to do it. She needed me." His voice softened. "She knew me. I thought...I thought I was dreaming."

So that's it then. He's in love with her. No wonder she's so screwed up. Hope understood the problem all too well and wouldn't take her new partner to task over matters of the heart. Being dead was tough enough on the soul. The music began, and she elbowed Sam gently.

"Pay attention now, it's time. You just watch. Let her fall into it." It was not the most auspicious moment, but Hope took what she could get, knowing she had no say over scheduling.

. . .

PERFECTLY HIGH, a little drunk, and no longer concerned about the border between the two conditions, Jack drifted away from the loud conversations overlapping around the table of acquaintances and customers. Hope glided up beside him, leaned a long thigh against his upper arm, and rested her hand on his bare shoulder.

Come on, Jack. Heed me now. She breathed a chill sigh onto his gold earring. He turned his head toward the cool wisp of contact and saw Anna sitting at the bar, her backside to him, her hair tumbling down her back in an unfashionable horsetail, sandals shucked to the floor under the stool.

Hope whispered to Jack from her heart hoping he would hear her this time.

That's right, cher, there she is. Go on now. Go get her. Hope stood tall, let her gaze linger on Jack's face for a moment, then glided back through the crowd on the dance floor to stand beside Sam.

Sam asked, "It's that simple?"

Hope snorted and shrugged. "This part, maybe. That boy thinks with his dick. But then what boy don't?" She laughed and jabbed Sam in the chest with a sharp elbow.

He blushed deeply but gathered his dignity as best he could. "Madam, I'm happy you find fun mocking me, but I was preserving my purity for my future wife as the Scriptures instruct."

"More's the pity," she said, dryly. "Now I know why they gave you this job."

"First of all, who are *they*?" he shouted. "Are we agents of the Devil or the Lord? I'm so confused."

Hope shoved him. "Shush with your questions for now. This ain't about you tonight. Or me. It's about them." They watched Jack come up behind Anna, hesitate, then cup his large hand under her elbow and bring his mouth close to her ear. She leaned back into him to listen.

"She seems to like him, but I can't fathom it," disapproval carving a groove between his eyes. "He looks to be a lout and a pirate."

"He's all that and worse but be grateful she's willing. This could go quicker than I thought. She's as much a savage as he is. Maybe more." Hope shifted her attention to Sam who was biting his lower lip, his eyes narrowing as Anna eagerly towed Jack through the crowd to the dance floor.

"You better get over that jealousy, Sam. That's not going to help matters, 'specially when he talks her out of her panties." Knowing Jack as she did, she figured 'round midnight.

"Out of her what?"

"Never mind, cher." She sighed, knowing she'd have to hold him back herself when the time came.

From what she could tell so far, their mission, whether Sam liked it or not, was to make the match between Anna and Jack. Why was Sam being so obtuse? And her big question, why did the Powers That Be want Anna and Jack to find each other? Matchmaking, if that's what this was, had not been a part of her experience, before or after she was dead. How could she get things done right with only slivers of information and roadblocks like Sam? She began to get the feeling that she'd been slipped into a management position without being told.

~O~

S1:E1

S omeone was fighting for her life and losing.

Jack cut across the deserted avenue at a trot. He was running late. A streetlight jittered on and cast his shadow across the pavement and up the mossy stone wall like a black beacon zeroing in on the action. Far louder than her muffled cries, the victim's psychic screaming doubled Jack over the moment his foot hit the cobblestone sidewalk. *So close. Stop it. Gotta try.* His brain was splitting with the fury and pain of her terror when the silent shrieking stopped and fell away like a feather drifting down into a well. Then one word. *Mama.*

It's what they all said.

It might be too late to save her, but it wasn't too late to stop the killer. There was no time to think about why, even though *Why?* was becoming the soundtrack of his consciousness lately. The question like a deep-toned bell in his chest. A vibration that had to be stilled by action. More than a calling, he was compelled. No feelings of sorrow or anger. Certainly, no remorse.

Jack hit the chest-high stone wall in two steps, gripping

the rough capstones to keep from falling over into the brush and trash on the other side. *Or was it a steep drop?* He didn't know this part of the park that well. It was raw out, even for the day after St. Patty's. He could see his breath and the stones were wet.

Letting himself down the inside of the wall silently, he found the brush dense, but not impenetrable. He went down on all fours and crawled toward a moving darkness that was only visible as a void in the low-level city glow on the other side of the bushes. Through the branches and leaves her white hands seemed to reach for him—palms up, fingers slightly curled—like flowers quivering involuntarily. She was gone.

He inched forward through a gap in the old laurels until he was so close, he could read her palm. Her scalp showed white in a zig-zag part. The paleness of her forehead and nose already waxen. Beside her in the grass, her broken glasses reflected the jagged skyline. Jack pictured her in a library, her prim, dark cardigan buttoned to the top. Her fingernails were short, cut that way on purpose, perfectly pink. The man on top of her was thrashing and moaning in his drug-addled rut, oblivious to Jack's presence.

Jack eased the weapon, still wrapped in soft paper, from his pocket. A gift from Chang that very morning—elegant, simple, and lethal. He wanted to ponder the significance of the timing, but this wasn't the time.

Sorry sweetheart, but at least there's this. He tucked the handle into her cupped fingers, closed his large hand over hers firmly, and swung the tool hard in a short, tight arc that ended at the man's temple. The impact triggered a spring-loaded spike that flashed out of the wooden handle and plunged deep into the rapist's brain. The man grunted and collapsed on the girl like a plug had been yanked from a socket, cutting off the electric pig vibes he was broadcasting. Jack wanted to push him off her, but the scene needed to speak for itself.

He scanned the short meadow and the path beyond, not twenty feet away. Nothing and no one so far. A streetlamp glowed from behind a bend in the path, making the darkness here more complete. Still on all fours, he leaned over the dead and plucked a thick billfold from the man's jacket and slipped it into his own. He gazed down on the victim's upside-down face for a moment, then gently nudged her eyes closed with the back of his little finger, repressing a fleeting urge to kiss her on the forehead.

In the arms of the angels now.

Backing out through the shrubs and over the wall, he paused to see if anyone was coming from either direction before easing down to the sidewalk. A block away, he ducked into a doorway and checked the billfold.

The first thing he saw was the thin gold badge. An assistant district attorney, according to a business card. Under the badge flap, three flattened foil packets of white powder. His fillings hurt just touching them. Large bills. Over a thousand in cash. Another few blocks and Jack found a payphone.

"Julio."

"Yeah, who wants him?"

"Got your camera?"

"Always. Who is this?"

"Central Park West, over the wall at 89th. High profile. Make sure it gets to the Post."

"I'm on the way. Who is..."

Jack hung up. A few more blocks uptown, he wiped the wallet clean and slipped it through a sewer grate, badge, and all. He kept the cash.

An unexpected wave of exhaustion came over him and he sat down heavily on a stoop and lit a cigarette. He bowed his head in prayer. *Seriously, guys. How long do you think I can keep this shit up and what difference does it make, really? I gotta get the fuck out of this city.*

AND GO WHERE CHER? Hope felt sorry for Jack right now, but she was sure he'd find a way to aggravate her before the night was through. She leaned against the lamppost on the sidewalk in front of him, the crystal beads on her dress and the whites of her eyes glittering in the moisture that hung in the air. Rain so fine it wouldn't fall. Her long arms and legs and the perfect oval of her face shone as shifting fractures between the darkness and the streetlight. She didn't feel the cold and damp anymore, yet, out of old habit, she pulled the fringed silk shawl around herself in a comforting hug. The thought of leaving the city worried her, but she knew that she would have to follow him.

"Become his shadow" were her marching orders. There was nothing for her to do until the time came. Would she know it when it did? No one had all the answers. *That poor girl in the park. Won't she be astonished when she figures out what dead is?*

And now this trouble. The city had become lousy with crazy, coked-up motherfuckers like the one he just left dead in the park. Jack used to be fun to follow, a party boy, but since he'd come home from the Navy, he was getting worn down by people who were opaque to him, toxic. Their selfish evil endangered all. Every block she and Jack walked in Manhattan together sported three or four souls lit up like sparklers, their brains, or what was left of them, like rats in a wheel, running to see when and where the next score would come from and how sweet it would be when it arrived.

She smiled grimly, remembering her own last days. Days of soul hunger, always the bottomless wanting. And finally, the wanting over. At least her drug had left her passive. Somnolent. Dead inside before the fact of it actually happened.

These fools were possessed, soulless. Any limits they ever had to their depravity vanished in the face of their need. Nothing was out of bounds. Of course, no one else saw them this way but Jack and her. He could kill the needful day and night and not make a dent. The city was deeply infected by the mid-seventies, and nobody seemed to care. Everyone was having too much bright and shiny fun except Jack.

Hope wondered about the women Jack fucked, the party girls, brittle with plastic surgery and Cover Girl, anxious and ornery in some never-ending competition that he couldn't be bothered to fathom. They were hollow in a way that no amount of Jack could fill. He didn't take advantage; they scratched each other's itches and that had been the sum of it until just recently.

Jack flicked the cigarette into the street and shook himself like a dog. The night was young, and he had deliveries to make, then the luxury of a little short-term oblivion. Hope fell into step behind him as they made their way back uptown.

The next day, Julio's graphic, black-and-white photos didn't make the front page or even the second. Jack frowned over the newspaper in a coffee shop. The story on page three alluded to the female victim possibly having ties to some underworld connections. Pure bullshit, of course. He hoped her family would sue the publishers for defamation of character. *She was a librarian, for Christ's sake.*

The larger issue was that the man he'd stuck a spike through was a special assistant DA on the Mayor's drug task force. Jack sighed, "Of fucking course he was." He snapped through the pages to find the rest of the article. The streets would be hot for a while. It was a good time for a vacation in the country.

He was deep into the sports pages when the waitress sat down across from him. She lit a cigarette, slipped off one white clog, and tucked her stockinged toes between his legs. He looked at her over the top of his sunglasses and smiled. She was cute. Hell, she was warm, but he liked the coffee here and knew that women were a little harder to get rid of than a dirty sock or a handful of Kleenex. He had a busy day ahead.

He reached down and caressed her foot before removing it from his crotch. She pouted and went back to work. He left her one of the fifties he'd lifted from the detective's wallet as a tip.

~O~

S1:E2

APRIL 1974

The heavy garage door swung open silently thanks to the care she'd taken with the hinges and springs—grease spread thickly on any joint capable of noisy complaint. The sound of the car starting was another matter, but before Ray could get out of bed and down to the garage to interfere, she'd be a mile away. Fuck the consequences in the morning. No matter how much he thought he controlled her, it was none of his business when or where she chose to drive her car. Ray wouldn't say anything about it the next day, just as long as she was back before he woke up. As if it never happened.

BEFORE SHE COULD EVEN SEE over the wheel, Anna wanted to drive. Everyone called her Bea back then, short for Annabea, the name she'd been given in the river by her mother when the church wouldn't have either of them. When she was two, she would stand on the driver's seat of her Uncle Murph's old Ford pickup and pitch a fit because she couldn't get it to go. He would get in and shove her aside saying, "Sit down, shut up, and pay attention. Any fool can drive."

Then he would reach under the dash, twist some wires around—the keys long since lost—curse and tromp the pedals. The truck would grunt, fart, and chug to life, a giant behemoth, slow and uncertain, then faster and more powerful, like a bull in a full suit of rusting armor, only this one wouldn't stomp you to mush given half a chance. This beast could be commanded. She wanted that power. That magic.

Weekday mornings she would beat Murph out to the truck, climb up the side and through the open window like a circus chimp and stand, pounding her sticky little fists on the Bakelite wheel, screeching at her impotence. Murph would look through the open window, polishing his glasses on his shirttail, feigning indifference. "I got all day, little girl. We ain't going nowhere 'til you quit it."

She stopped the noise, but held her ground, glowering at him darkly from under a nest of tawny curls, one of the pink bows Tam tied into them hanging askew, the other missing. He peered at her. "How did you get so dirty?" Tam had just set her down in the dooryard, steps away, clean enough for church.

After a ten-second showdown, she dropped to her butt and scuttled over to the passenger side, folded her grubby hands in her lap, looked up at him and grinned, all teeth and contrition. Murph studied her suspiciously. Tam was right. This child would have her way with the world and everyone in it, and it would always be on her terms, none of them simple or easy. Life would be hard and lonely.

TWENTY-FOUR YEARS LATER, it was a good night for a midnight ride. Death usually came along. Sometimes he crowded her, put his arm around her and copped a feel. Whispered in her ear that all she had to do was close her eyes. Sometimes he hung onto the door handle for dear life, seatbelt cinched tight. Tonight, she left without him.

It was cool and clear, the moon new. She knew how she was probably going to die, just not when, but she hoped it wouldn't be tonight. There was something in the cards about tomorrow, but not enough of a something to wear a seatbelt over.

Some night, though, she knew she'd crest a poorly banked grade and feel all four tires tell the asphalt, "We surrender." For spite, she'd lean harder on the gas as the ripples of pleasure started between her legs, sparkling through her, flashing up into her heart the way summer lightning jumped from cloud to cloud, never looking for the earth.

It would happen as her hands gripped the wheel at ten and two, spine arched with pleasure, the car throbbing under her like a wild, living thing. One or another of the tires would find some kind of crap on the pavement—a chrome lug nut, big as a fist, tossed off by a highballing semi, or a small, freshly dead fox hankering for revenge—and the Chevelle would spook and shy, spin twice, hit the gravel verge, flip once, and cleave a greasy telephone pole in two, ten feet off the ground, taking out service in the rural area for miles in either direction. The conflicting g-forces of the flip would sever her spinal cord from her brain at the base of her skull, and she'd die mid-orgasm. Who could argue with such perfection? Surely this was how the most powerful ghosts were made.

But not tonight. Something was coming. The Wheel of Fortune was turning.

Tonight, she cursed at the tires, "Bear down, you lazy bastards. Bite!"

The slew corrected, the SS hunkered down and settled into a smoother whine on another long, straight stretch, RPMs holding. No redlining tonight. The thunder of the engine and the road, the physics of speed and gravity all moved her the way no man ever had. Everything was working like the well-oiled rocket she was riding. She didn't have to do a thing but drive and didn't need to do the math to know that she had more than enough road to get her there.

This was the only time and place in her life fully under her control. *Suicides and their foolish last gestures of imagined power. Take it to the limit indeed, but not tonight.* There was no music and no companionship on this night ride. Well beyond the reach of the Chevy's headlights, the Pleiades were flirting with what might be the horizon. She was almost there.

~O~

Something was different about Jack. His playfulness was gone. It was like he was trying to fuck her right through the bed, not so much rough as single-mindedly insistent. Like he was looking for something and trying to find it with his dick. His urgency might make her come if she could stop thinking about that expensive leather bag for a minute. It wasn't her first go-round with Jack, but she knew it didn't matter who she was. He came to the party looking to get laid, and she was sitting on the steps smoking a joint when he walked in. It would be a good way to pass an hour.

He'd sat down on the step below her and took the joint from her fingertips. She smiled at him, took his hand in hers and clutched his thumb like a teat, milking it. "Junie, right?" was all he said, and she was happy he remembered her name, dismissing the question in his voice as her imagination.

He wrapped his arms around her, lifted her off the stairs, and dragged her through the first open door with a mattress on the other side, kicking it closed behind him. They were down and naked in minutes and Jack was all business, touching and nipping her everywhere, lingering tenderly over a bruise on her hip before nudging her thighs further apart with his knees and boarding her. He made noises when he fucked; not grunts of effort, but rumbles and bits of melody like he was following the gallop of a song.

He took her face down, one hand gripping the edge of the mattress and the other wrapped around her chest, a small breast lost in the palm of his hand. Drenched in his sweat, the wet edges of her pale skin where he wasn't covering her prickled with chills.

He'd be a great drummer, she thought as she started to feel that blue light gathering in the pit of her stomach where he was rocking her.

"Jeez, Jack, what's the rush?" she panted, the knuckles of her toes scrubbing small circles on the sheets. He answered by taking her wrists in his hands and pulling her arms up over her head, stretching her out tight as he bowed her even harder. Her head turned so she could breathe, his mouth right next to her ear.

"Give it up," he gasped.

At the sound of his voice, she did, sizzling under him like meat on a grill. She clenched on him as he went thicker inside her, coming in hard thrusts as he rolled over onto his back, pulling her with him, staked on him, running his hands up and down her torso, clutching like a blind man groping for loose change.

Junie went limp and lay draped across him like a thin blanket of flesh. She smiled, knowing he would take her shopping first thing tomorrow. That red purse. He did it for Emily, what, two weeks ago? Those great fucking boots that the dumb bitch lost at a concert somewhere. It was what Jack did after fucking you. The presents. Everyone said so.

Hers was the first in a string of disappointments all over the city.

~O~

T he first week of school was over and it was still July hot. By the time Annabea pushed her bike to the crest of the hill, sweat was running out of her hair, and she wished she'd listened to Tam and worn a hat. The blue Columbia bike was full-sized, much too big for her, but she could get on it from a stop if there was anything she could mount from. Getting off was always a matter of speed, timing, and gravity. She had her things in her lunch box, and a library book, and no one to account to until dusk.

All week she'd been surrounded by swarms of older children on the verge of tears, hysteria, or violence, and she was exhausted with the effort of keeping everyone's sad cooties out of her head and paying attention to the new teachers and the endless rules. She would not be seven until the end of October and they had put her in with third graders who were still struggling with Dick and Jane while she was making short work of Huck Finn. Being alone on a country road was as good as it would get for her for a while.

The Old Post Road skirted the eastern edge of town with a gentle, half-mile downhill grade that leveled out and let bikes coast all the way to the dilapidated covered bridge that took fifty rumbling feet to cross a brook that was more rock than water this late in summer. The oiled dirt road had sunk deep between mossy rock walls and old-growth trees that had braided their crowns together overhead to create a cool, green tunnel that ended at that bridge. Weeds took a chance on growing on the centerline of the road, there was so little traffic.

The roadbed across the bridge had been refurbished with new timbers in recent years, but the walls were derelict. Rotted boards had fallen away, and sunlight streamed through the gloom in blinding spears. Bats roosted in the dark of the eaves. Nothing more than single railroad ties kept people from driving over the edge on either side and the bridge was so narrow that only one vehicle at a time could pass through.

Annabea had already passed top speed and was coasting up to the bridge when the front tire hit a loose rock hard enough to kick the bike out from under her and send her flying over the basket and broad handlebars to land flat in the dirt and gravel. She came in hard like she was stealing home plate, arms outstretched, the bike tumbling over her to crash into the first wooden upright of the bridge hashed with the evidence of previous bad judgments. *Better the bike than my head.*

Pain fired in a dozen places at once as she rolled onto her back trying to catch the breath that the fall knocked out of her. She landed just inside the mouth of the covered bridge and could see up into the rafters. Bat guano sprinkled the roadbed, and she could see their eye-shine as they woke up and craned their necks to see what the commotion was about. Not enough to fly out into the daylight.

Her hands and bare knees stung hotly, and her ears were

ringing. After a minute spent gasping for air, she sat up and took stock of her injuries. Her palms and knees were scored and bleeding and there were a few bits of gravel embedded in the heel of her left hand. It hurt to take a deep breath. Fat drops of blood pattered onto her hands and down the front of her shirt. With grimy fingers, she found a gash just under the point of her chin and she pressed the back of her hand against it to stop the bleeding. Somehow, the worst cut didn't hurt.

She looked back up the long slope of the road. The top of the hill was a glowing speck a mile away, and she gave up the idea of pushing the bike all the way back. Forgetting about her chin, she stood up gingerly and, finding that everything worked, picked the bike up from the dirt, and dragged it into the full sun. The wire basket was bashed tight around her lunchbox and the book. The front tire was flat and off the rim. She leaned it tight against the rock wall. Murph would have to come with the truck.

The sound of a vehicle entering the far end of the bridge, rumbling over the boards too fast startled her, and she shrank back against the bike and the stone wall even though there was plenty of room for a car to pass a pedestrian. She recognized the maroon Buick as it rolled by, and she prayed that somehow the driver hadn't seen her. The car came to a dust-boiling halt a few car-lengths past her, and she could see the man's eyes in the side-view mirror.

Her foolish imagining that if she didn't move, he couldn't see her, gave way to fear, but she still didn't move. Couldn't move, even when he began to back so slowly, she wasn't sure the car wasn't just rolling back on its own and any second he would put his foot down hard on the gas and peel out, spewing her with more gravel. But no, it kept rolling back, fat tires silent in the oily track, until she was face to face with the driver, her fear confirmed. Murph said he was a bad egg. After observing him stubbornly pester the waitresses at the diner, Annabea suspected he was worse than Murph knew.

She grinned at him and said, as casually as she could, "Hey, deputy." She was trying to pretend that this would be a routine exchange of greetings and he would go about his business, but she had forgotten how she looked.

Deputy Marcus Waterman stared at the girl half in horror and half in annoyance. "Jesus H. Christ, girl. What the hell happened to you?" He was out of the car, leaning in to reach for the radio handset when he remembered he was driving his own Buick and there was no radio. It would be months before his suspension was up and he'd be back in a county vehicle on patrol. He lifted his uniform hat and clipboard from the front seat and tossed them carelessly into the back. He'd just left the radio car at the station and was still burning with anger and embarrassment.

Another damned skirt had complained about him getting fresh, and he'd been warned before. In front of God and everybody, Sheriff Dunlap had said, "You're going to have to get used to the idea that you're not God's gift to women, Marcus. And take that damned uniform off!"

Thirty days without pay. They'd taken his badge and his gun, but he'd taken his throw down from his locker, folded it into the morning paper and strolled right out of the station house. The gun was small, bought for cash in a pawn shop his first week on the job. The sergeant called them "just in case" guns. Things happened, even in small towns. He dropped the weapon and the paper on the front seat of his car like any other morning, only today he wouldn't be taking his paper to the diner.

The bitches.

Looking at the injured child distastefully, he reckoned that his day could still turn around. Getting this brat home quickly might earn him some points with the Sheriff. Maybe even get him reinstated. Was she an idiot? Brain-damaged? She had still not said anything.

He stood by the open car door and gestured impatiently. "Well, get in and I'll take you home. Christ, what a mess." Blood dripped from her chin and he pulled a handkerchief from his back pocket and took a step in her direction. "Here now, don't be bleeding on my damn seats."

Annabea tried to back up but fell back against the bike and realized there was nowhere to run. He'd angled the tail end of the car to the bridge when he stopped, trapping her in the tiny triangle of space between the rock wall, the car and where he stood at the open door.

In a flat tone he'd heard from women all his life, this grubby little girl said, "No!" and an involuntary spark flared in his throat. "Get in the god-damned car," he yelled, grabbing her by the wrist, almost lifting her off her feet.

Inside the stuffy car, she scrambled across the seat to get away from his touch. His anger, her resistance, the blood and, most damningly, his cruel grip on her forearm, unleashed a cascade of memories in him that hit Annabea harder than her fall from the bike. She was unprepared and couldn't fend off his thoughts.

That girl from the bar, how he hit her and hurt her right here on this very seat. He pulled off her clothes and mashed her down with his body even though she was choking and crying. She screamed, but he crushed her between the seat and the door, his hands so tight around her neck that he felt her bones disconnect. How he'd dragged her out of the car right here on the bridge and shoved her through the broken planks down into the river.

Annabea heard the sound of the woman's skull hitting the big rock before she slid into the rushing water. He'd stood there and had a smoke as he watched her body circle twice then sink.

Annabea pushed herself up against the passenger door and clung to the fat armrest, her eyes fixed on the knob on the glove box because she couldn't see over the dash. She clenched her teeth to keep from crying but couldn't stop herself from shaking.

"Take it!" He tried to jam his handkerchief into her hand, and she started shrieking. He backhanded her across the face, and she clapped both her hands over her mouth to stifle herself. Staring in disgust at her blood on his hand, he spit-cleaned it with the handkerchief, then threw the bloody cloth to the floor. He slammed his door shut and hit the gas hard.

Annabea couldn't hide from his history, the bedtime stories he told himself. Now she knew why one of the older girls in her school had dead-looking eyes and wouldn't talk to anyone. How he made Ella get in his car on her way home from school, and when he was done with her, he told her that her little sister was next if she told on him.

Now his attention was on her the way a snake watches a mouse, and she was too afraid to make sense of what would come next until the rich voice in her heart said, *Not like the mouse, Annabea. Snap out of it!*

She scrambled to her knees on the seat to see where they were on the road and pulled on the door handle with every intention of jumping, but he grabbed her by all the thick, curly hair on one side of her head and pushed her head down to the seat beside him.

"You've gotten to be a whole lot more trouble than you are worth little bitch!" He slammed on the brakes and peered into the rearview as the dust slid past them. That's when she knew for sure he meant to kill her and she calmed herself, a plan in hand.

Then, in the hollow, panic-prone spaces of his head, Marcus heard a woman's voice. *They know what you've done, Marcus. What you did to that girl. All those girls. You've been stupid and now they know and you're gonna pay!*

Annabea covered her mouth, unsure which would come out, a scream or a laugh. Marcus sat bolt upright in the seat, tightening his grip on her head. She knew the voice she was hearing inside—the same voice he was hearing—would be her grown-up voice, the proof that she would live through this. The voice that gave her courage. She slipped her hand from her mouth to cover her ear.

They're coming for you, Marcus. Run! He whined a desperate moan and cranked the wheel over and back, three points, turning in the narrow road to go back the way they had come, back to the bridge. He slowed as he approached; the boards creaking as the heavy car pulled even with the gap in the wall. He looked down at her and said, "All this trouble just because I wanted to help a little girl out." He truly believed he was the one put out, the one suffering, and he seethed with the injustice of it all. He lifted her up from the seat by her hair and said, "You know..." and she shot him. Twice.

She'd curled her left hand around the gun to keep it from jamming into the side of her face when he first pushed her head down and she pulled the spongy trigger with the stubby barrel jammed right up against his hip.

The blast and stink of the shots deafened her and made her gag. One bullet skipped off his hip bone and tore up through his gut and right lung, the other went straight on through him to lodge in the car door. His blood didn't know where to gush first. He screamed and let go of her hair.

She pulled back on the door handle with her sneakered foot just as Marcus hit both pedals hard with both feet, the engine and brakes straining at odds. The big Buick spun a quarter circle inside the bridge, the ugly grin of the chrome bumper shearing through the dry wooden slats like paper. Her door swung wide, hinges cracking, and she was spewed out into the road to another hard landing, this time on her butt, her teeth clacking hard on her tongue, the stubby gun beside her on the boards specked with bat shit.

The car wedged sideways on the bridge, the power to the rear wheels gaining over his spasmodic pressure on the brakes. Rubber burning, the car climbed over the retaining timbers, splintering more flimsy side boards as it plowed out into space. Marcus turned to look at her through the open door, one hand clutching his side, the other still gripping the wheel, his face a broken mask of fear and fury. She looked right back at him, expressionless, making sure he saw her eyes before she scrambled to her feet to get clear of the spinning rear tires grinding air in her direction. He fell forward over the wheel, the small transfer of weight just enough to carry all two tons of steel over the side and thirty feet down to the streambed below.

She scrambled to the edge of the hole and lay flat, looking down on the Buick. It had landed on its wheels under the bridge, more on the rocks than in the water. Smoke from the engine turned to flames all along the underside of the car. She listened to him scream for a minute, cocking her head like she was trying to place an unfamiliar bird call until there was a muffled explosion under the car, and she fell back from the edge as pieces of debris hit the deck under her and arched smoking through the air. The lazy bats finally took exception to the disturbance and flew in a chittering swarm out the far end of the bridge, flicking through the acrid smoke. She toed the gun over the side into the growing flames.

ANNABEA WAS PUSHING her flat-tired bike a mile beyond the bridge when a volunteer fireman from the next town over stopped and picked her up. He was okay. Despite appearances, she was cheery. "Got a flat, had a wreck" was all she told him.

He put her bike in the bed of his pickup and said, "We got a call that the covered bridge burned up. It's over and done with by now, but I thought I'd have a look-see. If we can get across, somebody from the BFD will fix you up, get you home. If we can't, we'll go the long way round. You're a mess, young lady." He gestured for her to lift her head so he could see the wound but made no attempt to touch her. "Might need a stitch or two."

He was what Murph called a speechifier. Annabea nodded. "Won't be the first time," and went on to prattle about the three stitches she got in her shin last summer when she let go of the rope swing at the reservoir too soon, taking herself and the conversation anywhere in time away from the covered bridge. *Had they looked over the side yet?*

She smiled and stared out the window down the leafy green tunnel. Inside, she was still and hardened. The memory of the grown-up voice of herself felt like Christmas Past and Future rolled into one. Like a custom-made suit of armor.

Life brought lessons, and she was a quick learner. If you

knew what was coming before it got there, there were always ways of getting away from trouble. Getting ahead of it and even turning it on itself.

~O~

The word "fight" carries like the stench of death as the combatants square off inside a ring of looky-loos; the same scene repeated in schoolyards, playgrounds, and vacant lots all over the world, every single day.

This fight was on the street corner across from Holy Spirit. Some goody-goody had banged on the office door and ran. Father McLeod strode out to see what the commotion was. He crossed the street and stood at the edge of the ring of children who were too engrossed in the action to notice him. The priest, who was also the principal, watched without speaking, knowing that it would all be over in moments.

A kid, dark red hair, face spangled with freckles, is a full head taller and twenty pounds heavier than his opponent. The smaller boy has a cut over one swollen eye and bruises already showing on his arms. He's taken more hits than he's landed, sticking, and jabbing over and over with his right fist, knuckles raw. He holds his left hand back and away as if something precious was locked in his fist. Despite his injuries, a hint of a smile was driving his opponent into a rage.

Father McLeod had begged Chang to teach the boy karate or something, but Chang had refused, saying, "And have him kill someone? No. Let him find his own way." He recalled finding Jack, maybe four or five, and two of the youngest novices crouched on the floor of his study one afternoon, the black and white TV turned to The Mickey Mouse club. The trio seemed to be taking morality lessons from a singing cartoon cricket called 'Jiminy'. TV wasn't all bad. Jack had a strong, if oddly skewed, moral compass.

Why does he always wind up in fights with the older ones? the priest wondered as he stood back and let things take their unnatural course. Jack was already bleeding, but the fight would end quickly with the older boy face down in the dirt. If he were a betting man, he'd put it all on Jack.

Up until a glancing shot to his mouth, Jack had been all tease and tap, up on his toes like that heathen Cassius Clay, dancing to some devilish beat—right, right, a tap or miss with the left. He ducked and covered up haphazardly, took a punch to the ribs, then returned twice as much, but the other boy was protected by a layer of blubber. Jack was thin as an alley cat, although Father McLeod knew he ate like a stevedore. Once Jack tasted his own blood, a cold ferocity took him over.

This fight had been coming since school began when gossip swirled and the weak knuckled under to the bullies, resigning themselves to being beaten or extorted on a regular basis. The rumor that orphan Jack slept in a storage closet of the Holy Spirit convent kitchen was the smell of blood that this bully and his cronies had fastened onto.

The older boy yelled, "Come on, you Dago bastard, stop playing like a puss..." he took viper shot to the mouth before he finished the insult. Word about Jack's parentage, or lack thereof, had gotten around and this newcomer wanted to make something of it.

The bully spat blood in the dirt and puffed himself up to finish Jack off, straightening up, squaring himself, but Jack was ready. Father McLeod clenched his own jaw and fists. Jack dished right after right, boring in while the bigger boy swung a series of roundhouses that would have been devastating had they connected. Jack ducked, then danced in close and drove an uppercut into the flabby gut, knocking the boy's wind away.

The priest held his breath as Jack loaded his left like a shotgun. *Now, Jack. Now!* A stunning left hook to the jaw put an end to it all. The bigger boy went down, and Jack stood back, blowing, bristling, but already calming himself. He'd endured a five-minute mauling just to deliver a three-punch combination he'd read about in a comic book, the moves laid out panel by panel; the hero defending a rather racy-looking female of dubious honor. The title of the comic that he'd confiscated from Jack just the day before was *The Left Hand of Death.*

The priest ordered, "Alright, alright! That's enough now." The crowd scattered, and the man stood between the two boys, the loser still sprawled on his back, catching his breath. Jack had cooled, his stinging fists hanging at his sides.

"I want you two to shake hands and put an end to this."

The bully struggled to his feet and spat, "I ain't shaking no dago bastard's hand and you ain't making me." He backed away from the priest, flipped them both the middle finger and took off down the block.

Father McCleod took Jack's face in his hand and turned

it side to side, assessing the damage. "Dago? Did you start that rumor?"

"No, Father."

"You couldn't have made your move sooner?"

"Where's the fun in that, Father?"

They crossed the street back to the rectory for some first aid.

That would be all from the fifth graders and maybe the worst of the sixth, Father McLeod thought. But it wouldn't really matter because Jack would leave soon for a private school upstate. He didn't know yet, and the priest worried about how he would take the change.

~O~

A nna needed to know how things worked right down to how the molecules shoved each other around. Now chemistry was ruined unless she could transfer out of this class.

Mrs. Teller was the only female science teacher, but it turned out that her thoughts were as bad as those of most of the men on staff. Anna was no longer astonished at the constant barrage of depravity from the adults and older students she was surrounded by daily. The sex was the least of it. It was the selfishness, the never-ending judgment people put themselves and others through, everything tinged with fear in all its flavors. It exhausted her and left her scabbed over with cynicism, fierce in her protection of self and those few she cared about.

Teachers rarely assigned seats, so Anna always tried to sit in the front row window seat no matter what room she was in—a relatively safe spot that minimized the distractions and gave her a view of the sky.

At first, the woman was all business, handing out a three-page quiz to find out what they had forgotten over the summer or never learned in the first place. A stalker, she walked around the room and looked over people's shoulders as they worked. There was no question of cheating. Anna was nearly finished with the second sheet when the woman hung her butt on the windowsill just behind her and started mentally working her way through the girls in the room one by one, visualizing their naked bodies, imagining disembodied breasts. The boys she ignored completely. She started stalking again.

Anna tried to warn Mrs. Teller off with the kind of imagery she used on men—visions of bloody, dismembered hands twitching on the floor—but it didn't seem to register. She was hunched over the test trying to focus on the last question when the woman tapped her on the shoulder, making her jump in her seat. Before either of them could speak, the teacher's nose began to leak blood down the front of her pale-yellow blouse. Mrs. Teller tipped her head back and pinched her nose as several girls rushed to hand her tissues from the box on her desk. The bell rang and Anna bolted from her seat, slapping her test face down atop the big desk on her way out the door.

If they only knew. The suck-ups.

SHE HEADED for her favorite hiding place; the south-facing wall at the back of the science building. Sun warmed, the lawn was turfy and steep. She'd dropped to the grass in her usual spot before she noticed a clutch of older boys gathered at the opposite corner of the building. At her intrusion, all but one of them melted away, leaving the strong odor of pot in their wake. She'd been dying to try it but knew no one well enough to ask.

Junior Odom eased slowly her way. The biggest football

player on the team, the one assigned to mug the opponents, loomed over her. One of only a handful of blacks in the school, Junior had always given her a measure of respect that outsiders extended to one another, even if it was unspoken.

"You gonna tell?" he asked, without threat. She was a nobody, far less than he was. Anna squinted up at him. The sun seemed to be shining out of his head. Like the drinkers at the Windsock, he was nicely insulated. She got nothing from him.

"Only if you don't share," she said, reaching out for the joint as if it was something she did every day.

He laughed a bass rumble and said, "Okay, you go on then, little sister. Stay out of trouble." He gave her the last third of a fat, nicely rolled joint, then eased around the same corner the other boys had fled by. She smoked it down to the last possible ash, burning her fingertips, then sat back against the wall to assess the effect.

With her eyes closed against the brightness, Anna was briefly lost in mapping the blood vessels of her eyelids. The sound of her own breathing was like the ocean washing the sands at low tide. Unsteady at first, she stood, bracing herself against the concrete wall. There was a distant bell. Day's end. She gathered her things and made her way back around to the front of the building, climbing the steep grade with deep strides because her legs had gone from rubbery to powerful. She felt the need to watch her feet and was head down when she reached the front walkway, now flooded with students reacting to the last bell.

"Watch it, dopey." A boy with bad skin grabbed her by the shoulders, backed her up to the building like she was a piece of furniture, and continued on his way.

Nothing! She got nothing from him. From any of them.

She stared at the stream of almost men and nearly women and, for once in her life, she wasn't feeling the backwash of their fears and anxieties, the emotional sparks that everyone sheds all the time. It was as if she was wrapped in a cocoon, high and safe from the storm.

There was a saltiness in her mouth; she realized she was tasting her own tears, and she hurried to wipe her face. As good as it was, she knew it was only temporary, the high giving her a glimpse of how it was for everyone else in the world—alone in her head with only her own thoughts and feelings to contend with. Knowing it was possible felt like the promise of Christmas.

The fuzzy, old-fashioned hoot of the Ford's horn pulled her down from the daydream. Murph's truck idled at the curb.

"Who's in the cooler, Murph?" Anna said as she climbed into the pickup, eager to establish their usual banter. She didn't want to have to explain away the fuzziness she was enjoying so much.

"Nobody you know," was her uncle's standard punchline.

The joke had been running between them since she was old enough to understand that the big, black and white rabbits they raised were not pets. Empty now, the big, metal bait chest in the back of the truck had been filled with ice and carcasses he delivered to a few restaurants in the area. Rabbit was going out of style and hauling the meat to market in the city wasn't worth the gas it took to get there.

To Murph, Anna seemed quiet and distant, and he felt his heart sink a little. He missed the happy, aggressively curious little girl she'd been until she crossed that mystery bridge into womanhood. Her ability had been a problem they'd coped with, then gotten used to when she was still a small child. Now she bore the burden alone, and he knew she wouldn't talk about whatever was troubling her. The truck had no radio, and the silence hung between them. Murph was good at changing the subject.

"What's that smell?" he said, although he was pretty sure he knew what it was.

"Some jerk burned something up in chem lab today. I gotta wash my hair."

"Uh, huh. That too," he said. "We'll talk about it later. You in a rush to get home?"

"No. Why?" Now, she was eager to change the subject.

"Rogan called this morning. The skiff is ready, but the trailer has a flat. We can put it in the water at his ramp if you don't mind rowing it back up to town. I'll pick you up at the dock. Get a shake at the diner." This got what he was after. When Anna smiled, it was like the sun coming up after a week of stormy weather. His old rowboat had been out of the water for repairs for a month, and he knew she missed her time out on the water. The solitude was a blessing for her.

"Hell, yeah." The high had lifted her and leveled out, spreading like oil on troubled water. She might be on her way down, but the prospect of being out on the water was as sweet.

Rogan's Bait & Tackle was at the southern end of the reservoir. From there it was a two-mile row back to where Murph and a handful of locals left their rowboats pulled up on the banks a short walk from town. He went inside to buy a chain and padlock. A new-looking boat might be too much temptation for someone. "Let them borrow someone else's boat this season." He paid cash and Rogan pulled the tagged oars out of a stack leaning in the corner.

The three men out in the parking lot had just made

Rogan's morning. His week, in fact, and he was beaming. "City fellas out there pissed off because I told them they couldn't put their motorboat on the reservoir. Jackasses. I told 'em, "hey, that's your drinking water and I didn't make the law." So, I rented them a rowboat and they paid cash for rods, reels, bait—everything dudes need to drown worms." He and Murph shared a laugh.

Through the screen, Murph saw one of the men say something to Anna, then one of them reached out as if to put his hand on her arm, but she backed away from him and Murph headed for the door. She came through it first, backlit by the morning glare. Anna was dressed like any high school girl in jeans and a peasant blouse she thought loose enough to hide her assets until a breeze wrapped the thin cloth around her body.

From outside, Murph and Rogan clearly heard, "...cock-teasing jailbait, that's what." The crude remark hung in the air, smoking like a brand.

Rogan went white and took a step toward the phone on the wall. Murph had ten feet of steel chain and a heavy Master padlock in one hard hand.

She put her hand on her uncle's knotted forearm. "It's alright, they're just ordinary assholes."

But it ain't alright! Murph thought. *She lives with this crap all day, every day!* He was furious and brushed by her to stand on the porch, but by then, the men had pushed off from the ramp and were drifting south in the direction of the dam. He watched as two of the men clumsily traded places, while the one at the oars cursed them both and struggled to keep the boat from tipping. Annabea and Rogan joined Murph.

"I warned them to stay away from the dam." It was easy to get caught in the current and swept over the spillway.

Murph composed himself for her sake and said, "Why don't we come back tomorrow and do this, little girl." He stared at the place where the aluminum skiff had gone around the bend out of sight.

Not anyone's little girl anymore, Anna put her hands on her hips and said, "No. Because I'm headed in the opposite direction and anyway, they couldn't catch me if they had a motor." She grinned fiercely. "And if I let every miserable prick, pardon my French, Mr. Rogan, upset my day, I'd never get out of bed in the morning." They knew she was right.

The two men killed another half hour with small talk before putting the skiff in the water and standing back to watch Anna put her back into the rowing.

Rogan said, "You better haul ass, Murph. She'll beat you back if you so much as stop for gas."

THE STATE POLICE rousted Rogan out of bed that night at midnight. He took them down to the shop where a police wrecker was already hooking up the fancy Wagoneer and powerboat the men had left locked up in his parking lot. He showed the cops the receipt for the rental and the gear they had purchased and learned that all three men drowned. The boat had been swept over the spillway a mile south of the shop.

The police never asked if anyone else had been around, and Rogan never mentioned Murph and Annabea. He and Murph had operated on the wrong side of the law together a few times back in their misspent youth. Answering questions that hadn't been asked was not something old friends did.

As the taillights of the cop car and the tow truck disappeared down the highway, he thought about the name

Murph had him paint on the stern of the rowboat. "Jesus Christ, Murph. Naming a rowboat is asking for trouble. What a pain in the ass."

He'd painted the name Annabea asked for in red enamel script across the width of the boat's transom. They had argued about the spelling, but she insisted on two 'S's. Said she had her reasons. He took a scrap of paper with the words 'Just Desserts' off the cork bulletin board, tossed it into the belly of the cold wood stove, and grumbled to himself about having to make an insurance claim for the lost rowboat.

~O~

S1:E7

SEPTEMBER 1971

The fall term was underway. A girl sat in a window seat on the second-floor common area of the dorm and looked out across the park-like campus. September was full-on, and a guy was rambling down the sidewalk with a wind-blown herd of red and gold leaves. 'bopping' would be the best way to describe his walk. Tight jeans, sunglasses, long brown hair tied down with a blue bandanna, struggling sideburns, and a wannabe porn-star mustache—he looked like all the guys in the band. As he passed by with his fists jammed in his pockets, shoulders straining the short denim jacket, she marveled at his ass.

"Somebody please tell me he's a student here." She opened the window wide to lean out and follow his progress, quashing her desire to throw a loud wolf whistle in his direction. Nice girls from Kansas didn't do that. Leering was bad enough. Her new roommate elbowed her aside, and Renata, a senior, joined them.

"A fine ass is the power behind the hammer," Renata said as she looked over their shoulders. "Who we talking 'bout?"

"Him."

Renata recognized Jack and snapped her gum thoughtfully. "Sorry ladies, he's not a student here, but you'll see plenty of him and maybe more."

She smiled to herself and thought about the night she'd spent tearing up the sheets with Jack just a few weeks ago. *Boy was ferocious in the sack.* How she'd come down to the front stoop the next morning in her silk robe looking for a rematch to find Jack passing a joint with the finest brother she'd ever seen. How Jack had introduced her to Earl as if she were visiting royalty and not Jack's most recent conquest. For one so young, Jack had style and Earl was looking more like a keeper every day.

"What do you mean?" Kansas said.

"This fine dude is our sweet Captain Jack, always holding, horny, and hung. Our preferred connection for pot, fresh from the city. All the dope you can smoke. Jack delivers, in more ways than one."

"He's dreamy." Kansas sighed.

Renata laughed. "Keep dreaming. He'll make the sale, fuck you silly, and never ask your name. You'll call out to Jesus, and he'll be gone before you're done twitching."

"Drugs? Really?" Roommate asked, blinking her way back to reality.

"Girls, wake up. This is college. Sex, drugs, rock and roll, and some education on the side. Maybe. Better get your birth control and your priorities in order."

Jack stopped to light a cigarette and flicked the spent match into the street.

Kansas squinted at him. "How old is he?" There was something unfinished about him.

Renata laughed. "Honey, Jack's still in high school, which is why you'll only catch him up here on the weekends. He's the devil's own, that one," but she was smiling when she said it. "Mm, mm, mm. Now that I think about it," she slapped at her jeans pockets, "Scuse me, ladies. I gotta see a man about some weed." As she dashed for the stairs she yelled, "Tell him to wait!"

Kansas and her roommate leaned out the window and both yelled, "Jack, wait!"

Jack stopped, looked up and flashed a dimpled grin up at them. "What's up, ladies?"

"Shit, but he's cute," muttered the roommate as they watched Renata hustle up to him.

He opened his arms wide, catching Renata in a hug with a kiss that turned into an impromptu dance to music only they could hear. One, two turns, he kissed her cheeks and slipped something into her breast pocket with a lingering caress. He slapped her on the ass smartly, turned and went on his way, never missing a beat, still grooving to his tunes. Renata looked up at the window and laughed with her tongue hanging out of her mouth. The girls shrieked and elbowed each other laughing.

IT HAD BEEN A GOOD TRIP, a two-grand weekend, but he was tired and all he wanted was a shower and a few hours of sleep. He'd thought about turning the key on Renata, but he knew there would be no rest if he stayed with her, so he kept on moving, heading for the train station. It would be midnight before he got back to school, and he'd have to sneak in the dorm window. It was getting to be a toss-up whether he'd be expelled before he graduated, but the private scholarship to Fordham was a lock, regardless. Whether he would actually attend was another matter. He was just too damn busy making money and partying.

The profits from this weekend would go for some wheels, something serviceable, the kind of car nobody looked at twice. He was going to need a car to keep working the 'burbs. Trains weren't enough. He'd also have to get a fucking driver's license eventually. More bureaucratic bullshit. He needed a base of operations, away from the city, from the hustle, the life. Things were getting hot. The list of people he needed to avoid was getting longer. *Could there really be too much sex, drugs and rock 'n roll? Nah.* Humming, he snapped his fingers and picked up his pace.

His thoughts returned to the aggravation at hand. There was a guy who needed his brand of personal attention, the permanent kind, and he'd let the man slip away. There were probably a lot of them, but this one had been riding the train with him on the trip up from the city. Jack had the bad luck of this crazy fuck taking the seat right in front of him several stops before he was due to get off.

The man looked like anyone's low-rent accountant, but Jack had been bored and eavesdropped on the man's thoughts. Uptight-looking straights were usually entertaining what with all the raging repressions they had going on. Reading the mental doings of total strangers was something Jack did to pass the time. Acting on his findings? Well, there's the rub. Jack appreciated Shakespeare's running commentary on the fucked-up-ness of the human condition.

This was how Jack discovered that the man sitting in front of him was a serial killer who specialized in choking old ladies with their own stockings and then screwing them while they were still warm if quite deflated. Elderly women alone in their homes. Most of them had hardly even fought back. This creep saw himself as the hero of their entire lives.

So far, there were seven victims that he bragged to

himself about, going on in his head with two voices, his own and a querulous female. His mother, most likely. She told him they all deserved it. He had a built-in cheering squad. After five minutes of the man's gruesome mental shit-show, Jack was sure it was not the guy's wishful thinking, and he got up and moved to the standing-room-only smoking car.

Fucking commuters.

There was nothing Jack could have done about the killer at the time. He'd indulged in a brief fantasy of dragging the man to the door and throwing him off the moving train, but there was no guarantee in that action. Jack patted the knife in his jacket pocket reflexively. He was trying not to do any freelance work, and he frowned thinking about his priorities. There just wasn't enough time to answer every call.

It had been a dry trip. No dope or pussy, no matter what, and there was certainly no time for flushing the gene pool. There'd been appointments at three different colleges and connections to be made that couldn't be changed or missed. His reputation and a lot of cash had been at stake. But, still, he nagged himself, he should have worked the guy in somehow.

The killer was on the run now, headed for Canada eventually. Jack knew the man planned to keep right on doing what he'd been doing, but the fool was so in love with himself he was bound to get careless sooner rather than later.

As Jack boarded the home-bound train, he resolved to drop a few anonymous tips to the cops in the towns where the murders had taken place. He had the names of the victims and the name of their killer. He would give the pigs something to do besides pester pleasure merchants like himself. Community service, that's what he was doing.

Jack sighed and consoled himself with the knowledge

that Chang had plenty of work for him. Paying work that spread the risk factors greatly. There would be no more giving it away, no more moral mandates from above. He was tired of answering the call for justice. Where was the payback? There was no shortage of deserving miscreants in Chang's business and the old man paid cash. He even handled disposal, a constant problem for Jack. *Can't just leave 'em lying around anymore.*

The conductor slammed the door open. Jack paid his fare, put his boots up on the opposite seat and settled in. He cupped his crotch and sighed, *Renata,* and thought about how dancing with her at a party last month had turned into an overnight fuck fest. Handing her off to Earl the next morning was the frosting on the cake. Jack loved it when it started with a dance. So did the ladies.

HIS SECOND SUMMER home from Graymoor, the dean sent a letter telling Father McLeod that he'd better make sure Jack had a job, something to keep him off the streets. Jack was trouble waiting to happen. One of the parishioners at Holy Spirit, a young widow, ran a dance studio and had asked the priest if he knew of any young men who would be interested in helping her give dancing lessons.

Father McCleod said, "At the height of disco, she teaches ballroom dancing, of all things." But it was in the neighborhood, and she assured him that Jack would learn manners that would take him far in life. So, for five bucks cash a session, Jack was drafted as a standby guy when there were not enough men to go around, and there never were. The majority of her clients were women. Brides-to-be dragged in their fiancées and often, their bridesmaids.

The first time Father McLeod brought Jack to the studio,

he was wearing bell-bottoms, sneakers, a dirty Holy Spirit t-shirt, and the shadow of a mustache that looked like dirt smudged over his bemused grin. He was happy because this gig looked more promising than delivering groceries.

Father McCleod told Connie, "He loves music so you should be able to teach him the basics and you'll be keeping him out of trouble for me. We're grateful, right Jack? Stand up straight." He left Jack to fend for himself.

Connie waited for the door to close behind the priest. She scowled and said, "Shit, it's a good thing most of my clients are short. Do you even own a suit?"

"No, ma'am," he muttered, eyes on his dirty laces.

"Never mind," Connie said, "We'll find something that works. Well, come over here. I won't bite. And no smoking before you come in here." She cuffed Jack on the side of the head. "Your pretty face won't do you no good if your breath is nasty."

Connie was in her late twenties when she lost her husband in Vietnam. Childless, she was determined to run a successful business rather than go looking for a replacement man and she had no time for distractions. She put on a record and was showing Jack some basic steps when he stumbled over his feet, his hardon catching her hip. She grabbed him between the legs and his face turned bright red.

"How old are you?" she demanded.

Jack managed a cracked, "Fourteen."

She stepped away from him and looked him up and down again. "Well, Mr. Big Surprise, these are paying customers, so you keep your wooden Indian off their baby baskets, if you don't mind. I'm sure you'll be the life of the party someday, but for now, I just need you to learn how to dance. Enough nonsense! Stand tall."

She took his sweaty paw in hers, gripped him by the waist and said, "Right now you're gonna be the girl, so I can teach you how to be the man." Once Jack relaxed, she knew Father McCleod was right. The kid was a natural.

Summer passed. The last student of the day had canceled, and she flipped the harsh fluorescents off, leaving only the after-hours neons burning red and purple in the windows. She put a scratchy copy of "Are You Lonesome Tonight" on the turntable.

Connie had nearly given up teaching Jack to waltz. Of all the steps they'd worked on, the simplest seemed to elude him. With Elvis doing the talking this time, Jack got it right for the first time, no false moves.

The song ended and the music was replaced by the muted sounds of traffic in the short, fragile twilight when the city takes a breath before the tumult of the day plunges into the chaos of the night. Jack kissed Connie softly and waited. Toe to toe, the energy that had been bridging the scant space between them held them fast.

She ducked her head and murmured, "Don't do that, Jack. You should be with girls your own age."

He put his lips close to her ear, breathing in her scent. He could hardly speak. "Girls my age don't know what they want."

She searched his eyes and rested her fingertips on the shadow over his mouth. *Is this a boy or a man?*

He moved his hand from her waist to her breast in a way that made her forget the question.

IT HAD BEEN a one-time thing with Connie. Something they'd look back at when they wanted to, a moment in each other's history. Although he didn't know it at the time, that moment set a pattern for Jack. Savor that first time with a girl or woman and make it special by making it the last time, a rule he didn't break until much later.

The memories, the sounds, and motion of the train took him under. With the bandanna pulled down over his eyes, arms folded across his chest, Jack slept the sleep of the innocent until the conductor crashed through the door an hour later bellowing, "Peekskill. Next station stop is Peekskill."

~O~

Murph let Anna drive his old Ford pickup to school when he wasn't using it, a rare treat. She'd been driving it around the farm since she could see over the steering wheel, so her skill wasn't his concern. It was the other assholes on the road he always worried about.

She'd lingered in the library doing homework after the last bell to let the first crush of students clear the halls. By the time she reached the parking lot, there were only a few cars left. The truck's front tire was flat. *Shitfire*, Tam's watchword. Anna looked around at nothing knowing that this would be up to her, and she opened and slammed the door just for some sound to cue her to action. Murph kept the jack and tools jammed up under the passenger seat. She was at the back of the truck bent over confirming that the spare was there when she heard a low whistle from a car on the opposite side of the lot. Anna straightened up and looked for the whistler with narrowed eyes.

Ray Cheverini, one of the last of the hoods in the school, was the leader of his mangy pack even though he'd quit the year before. He got out of the passenger seat of the old

Chevy hotrod and sauntered over to stand beside her, his hands jammed in his pockets, his eyes on the flat tire. From the car crusted with gray primer his buddies hooted and whistled. Ray gave them the finger with a menacing look, silencing them.

"I don't need any help," Anna said. She'd worn a skirt and blouse that day and was trying to figure out how she could crawl under the truck to free the spare from the cradle without putting on a free show for this pack of morons, but she was at a loss.

Ray squatted down beside her to check for the spare. "I can see that." He finally looked up at her and smiled. He was good-looking in that lean Italian way, still combing his hair back with something shiny while most boys went around sporting haystacks of hair. His hands, even his nails, were clean, and his aftershave drifted up to her.

"Well, what do you want?" *If he'd just get bored and leave, I could get on with it.*

"I'd like to watch you do it, but" he tapped the toe of her sneaker with one finger making her jump back out of his reach, "I can see you're not dressed for the occasion."

"Thanks for nothing Mr. Blackwell," she sniffed, folding her arms across her chest. His eyes had lingered too long there for her comfort. More baboon noises came from the waiting car. Ray stood up and didn't have to look their way to silence them. She wouldn't give him the satisfaction of asking for help.

He slowly brushed imaginary dirt from his knee, then his hands, and folded his arms across his chest mimicking her. "Looks like you got a dilemma. You can change it your-self and make me look like a chump while they get to check out your panties. Or you take my offer of a little help. In fact, I bet I can get it changed and neither one of us lifts a finger."

"A bet?" Anna cocked her head. Any betting held a chance of winning. "What's my end?"

"You get your tire changed and I take you out to see a movie and maybe get a bite."

"Can you get pot?" She had no intention of trading; it would be cash and carry only.

"Sure," he shrugged. "Whatever." He thought she was a bookworm and she'd caught him off-guard. Ray didn't get high, but he liked being around people who were. Liked proclaiming himself the one-eyed king in the country of the blind.

Fists on her hips, she said, "Alright, wise guy. Let's see you deliver."

Ray opened the truck door and gestured her inside like it was his royal coach and not her uncle's idea of solid wheels. "Now, do what I tell you. Keep your hands on the wheel and your mouth shut." She got in, resigned to let this bully have his moment, but secretly thrilled by his attention. His bossiness.

"Don't get an attitude, now," he added. "I'm gonna stand out here and watch. Sit tight!" She bit down on her indignation and did as he said. It would quickly become a bad habit.

Anna watched in the side mirror as he strolled back to the Chevy. He had long legs and a nice ass, but there was something she didn't like about the body language he used with his crew. The last thing she wanted to do was take a brush at what he was thinking, dwelling on. He was already making her anxious. Queasy. Guys were all the same, some worse than others. This one was predictable enough so far.

Ray leaned in the window and had a few words with the occupants. Four guys got out and returned to the pickup with him, all of them studiously ignoring Anna.

"Where's the jack?" Ray asked dryly.

"Under the seat."

As he came around the front of the truck, he smiled at her through the windshield, and when he opened the passenger side door, he leaned across the seat and whispered, "The next time I smile at you could you please just smile back?"

She made no reply. It may have been the last time he ever said 'please' to her.

He got the tools and slammed the door with more muscle than was called for and she stared straight ahead. He stood in her line of sight and watched the others changed the tire like a Daytona pit crew or thieves in the night. She clung to the wheel when they jacked the truck up and again when it dropped back down onto the spare. Ray stowed the tools back under the seat and slammed the door again. He popped up right outside her window startling her and making her yelp. "So. Tomorrow night. Seven." It wasn't a question.

Anna drummed her fingers on the steering wheel and said, "Okay." 'Thank you' did not seem to be in order.

"Now, remember what I said about smiling," Ray warned. He turned and swaggered back to the Chevy. The driver revved the engine and backed in beside the truck, Ray leaning out the passenger window with a big, theatrical grin spread across his darkly handsome face. She couldn't help herself. She smiled back. She was a high school junior who would be going out on the first date of her life.

They'd squared off then and there; she, daring him to be a gentleman despite his inflated ego and general selfishness. He, challenging her to act like his idea of a high school girl. Without either realizing it, they'd struck a deal.

To the world, Anna was the brainy type with poor social

skills and no fashion sense. To say she was considered unfriendly was generous. She was arrogant with a dash of hostility and that was exactly the persona she cultivated. Anna sat cynically alone until the day she took Ray's bet.

Ray squired her around like she was something special, telling her, "If you pretend you're hot, everyone believes it", but she quickly grew bored with him and his propensity for being right all the time. There was no denying he was good at people.

They went on dates and there was the obligatory necking and groping, but Anna drew the line there and Ray didn't seem all that bothered by her resistance. A sexual stalemate. She just wasn't all that inspired by Ray's self-centered, sweaty urgencies and was unable to imagine a payoff worth the indignity of sex. What did or didn't happen in private was nobody's business, but she found herself getting a measure of distant respect from her female class-mates and looks of scrutiny from the boys. She liked it, despite herself, and she liked that Ray, with all his limitations and false bravado, had brought her to a sense of social awareness.

Ray put on a show for Tam and Murph, but neither of them ever warmed to him and things got worse when he smugly wrangled himself a 4F. "My back," he'd said. There'd be no Vietnam for Ray Cheverini. He had more important things to do. He made good money working full time as an electrician's apprentice and had his eye on some kind of cockeyed future but never asked for Anna's input. She was focused on finishing school and expected the relationship to end when she left for college. Ray would be history and that was fine with her.

. . .

FALL HAD BEEN a long slog of cold and rain and she was feeling the weather. Bored and restless, her moods rubbed off on Ray making him surlier and more unpredictable. They went to the last home game of the season out of boredom. Rather than pay at the gate, only to leave after a short while, they sat in Ray's car at the far end of the field. He'd brought a six-pack of beer and forgot to bring any soda for her.

Anna opened a beer and took a timid sip. Ray laughed at her, and she gave him the finger. She knew she shouldn't drink beer. It hit her too hard and too fast. One beer and she'd be high as a kite for fifteen minutes, sullen for another fifteen, and out cold for an hour. Chugging most of it, she held up the can, burped, and said, "This'll be your fault for not bringing me a Coke, you cheap prick."

Ray grunted and snickered. At least they were alone. She was embarrassing. More than once he had to carry her out of parties and leave her passed out in the back seat of his car. He scowled and returned to the game trying to see where the team stood. Anna leaned forward to see what he was looking at and bumped her head on the windshield. Ray laughed at her again. "Dumb bitch! Sit back. I can't see."

Anna rubbed her forehead. "This is a waste of time. The other team is going to kill them." She hated football.

"What do you know about shit?" he barked. "You don't even know which end of the field is ours." It had been a winning season for the home team and Ray had bet accordingly. She didn't know about his gambling. It was none of her business. He'd spent a year hauling her around for show. With that rack, she had potential, but he was sick of her arrogance and lack of respect.

Her beer was almost gone and so was she. Tired of being mocked and dismissed, Anna made a grab for Ray's attention. She knelt on the seat and intoned, "Your quarterback is failing chemistry. He's worried about losing a scholarship. His girlfriend told him that she's pregnant, but he's not even sure it's his. He's a mess."

Ray took another sip of his beer and muttered, "You watch too much fucking television."

Anna giggled and stared at the field like it was something new and wonderful. There was a flurry of activity. The ball had been fumbled, again. The home team was losing.

Ray slapped his hand on the dusty dash, startling her. "How the fuck do you know all this?"

"Dennis ran right into me yesterday outside the chem lab." It had been a solid hit. Breaking all her rules, Anna told Ray about the encounter, and what she'd learned from it. The star player had caught her by the shoulders and lifted her to her feet. He cupped her face with a huge hand and apologized profusely before cutting across the lawn. No one could catch him. Today he was tripping over his own feet.

"What the fuck? He knocks you down, gropes you, and you what? Read his mind?" Ray sneered at her. "I told you, those soap operas will rot your brains." He leaned forward gripping the wheel, trying to focus on the game.

Drunk or high, she couldn't read anyone, but she leveled her gaze at him and said, "You, on the other hand, are boring." She waved a hand his way, dismissing him. "Always worrying about what people think of you. And if you didn't think about sex so much, maybe it will actually work someday."

Ray's face flamed. "Bitch!" He grabbed her forearm and dragged her across the seat, then shoved her away from him, and she scooted as far across the seat as she could, spilling the dregs of the warm beer down her legs.

His problem was something she'd learned about not long after they started dating. No sex was just fine with her. Sober, she knew better than to mention it, much less tease him about it. Drunk, she was happy to humiliate him.

Ray started the car and gunned it out of the lot. Anna grabbed onto the door handle wondering what would happen if she opened it at this speed. *Is this a physics problem I'm supposed to be doing?* She reached for another beer, but Ray slapped her hand away as she groped at the cans. He pulled behind an abandoned gas station, cut the engine, and sat staring off into the scrub as the engine ticked and cooled.

"Where are we?" Anna said her faced pressed to the glass. It was all she could do to stand up when he pulled her out of the car then muscled her into the back seat. With her feet still on the cracked pavement, she stared up at the upholstered rows of the headliner, thinking how it looked like a freshly turned garden. Ray reached under her skirt and yanked her panties off. She whined and curled away from his rough touch. He backed out of the car, looked around once more, and unzipped his fly. He wanted to punish her, once and for all, but his limp penis was as sulky and defiant as she was. He slapped at his own crotch in fury and frustration. The pain barely registered.

He leaned against the fender and smoked a cigarette, staring at her legs hanging out of the open door. One of her red knee socks was down around her ankles, her Keds dirty. *This is her fault. Nobody could fuck a sloppy drunk.* His litany of blame grew longer by the minute.

What if she really can do it? He'd seen it on TV and there was no proving it one way or another, but this was different. *This is happening live. Right here. My girl.* He'd lost $200 and cursed thinking how he was going to have to steal the money from his mother or wheedle it out of his father to pay the bookie. *If I only knew about that fucking loser before the game. That's her fault too, bitch. Hell, if this is real, she could be worth putting up with.*

It was near dark and starting to drizzle. He flicked the cigarette butt into the gloom, picked up Anna's legs and pushed her across the seat. She stopped snoring long enough to reach out and feebly fend off his touch as he tugged her sock back up her leg and her skirt down. *Girl needs a shave.* The rain drummed on the roof of the car as he drove off, running over her underwear.

~O~

L ater that week Jack got busted.

He'd gotten away with crimes that could have gotten him life in prison but farebeating on the Hudson Line would be his first actual arrest. There had been minor run-ins with the law before; stupid stuff like truancy, trespassing, fighting. Each time, he'd talked his way out of any serious consequences. This would be his first time in handcuffs, and he was surprised to find himself thinking that it was kind of inevitable.

He'd been traveling between Peekskill and Manhattan for over a year without paying a dime in fares. He moved between cars just ahead of the lazy conductor who'd long since decided that the railroad didn't pay him enough to do more than easy business with sleep-walking citizens who offered up their tickets to be punched without him even asking.

Then came the day the conductor was assigned to train a rookie; an angry young guy who had failed in his bids to be a cop, then a fireman. Train conductor was a sad fallback position. The rookie eyeballed Jack early while he was changing cars, then finally caught him slipping into a car three steps behind the head conductor.

In a loud voice that startled the sleeping passengers and nearly gave the conductor a heart attack, the rookie yelled, "Hey you, you're under arrest!" without really knowing if he had the power to do so.

Trapped between the two men with nowhere to go, Jack was just relieved that they hadn't caught him on his trip north because they would have found a whole pound of pot on him instead of the ounce he'd kept for himself. The breaks of the day. He used that gratitude to balance his fear of being caged. Confined. Jack was claustrophobic, and he knew he was going to be tested.

A beat cop on his way into the city for his shift put Jack in handcuffs and took him into the precinct satisfied that three-quarters of his day would now be consumed by processing a fare-beater. He could stretch out lunch to fill the rest of it.

On a gamble that the charge would be tossed, Jack refused to plead out and take the ticket. He was put in a holding cell until a probation officer could take him before a judge. At that point, Jack still had every intention of bolting. He had no ID on him so all they had was his name, which he'd given earnestly in a pretense of cooperation.

He waited all day in a large holding cell with what appeared to be the entire membership of a fraternity house brought in hours before him, all for public intoxication. Almost every one of the boys had thrown up at one point or another in the night and, as the morning wore on, lawyers sent by their parents came to retrieve them, each one more disgusted with his client than the next.

The population of the cell rose and fell as the hours passed and several newcomers—regulars who seemed to know one another—played poker, paper matches standing in for money. Jack stood by kibitzing near an unhappy giant, the name 'Door' stitched on his grimy jacket. He was a lousy poker player. Jack was bored and had had enough sitting and waiting. The room was getting tight. It was time to stir the pot. Reading the grubby giant and planting *'dumb-ass loser'* in his thoughts did the trick. He needed out of this box sooner than later; an improvised ruckus was the best exit he could come up with on short notice.

Door jumped up and grabbed Jack up by the front of his shirt and jacket and pinned him a foot off the floor against the bars of the cell. Jack crossed his arms over his face as best he could but seemed unnaturally relaxed for a guy about to take a beating. He said, "I told you he was bluffing, and you didn't listen to me."

Cards and matches scattered on the floor; the other players stood by to have their shot at Jack if Door didn't kill him first. Incredibly, Jack egged him on. "If you'd listened to me and played your damned hand, you'd be fat and happy, you dumb fuck." He was counting on Door's response. Someone was going to get hurt and it wouldn't be Jack if he could help it.

Door pulled back a ham-sized fist and aimed for Jack's face, but in the last second, a voice inside his head warned, *Behind you, asshole!* Door hesitated, then swung wide as he sneezed violently. Jack grimaced and twisted to get out of the spray as much as the blow, and Door's hand crashed into the bars as Jack kneed him in the vicinity of his balls. Howling in pain, Door dropped Jack and fell back into the onlookers.

This was a holding cell and overt violence was not

tolerated. The guards started bellowing from down the corridor, calling for reinforcements. The decibel level in the room tripled. Jack scuttled to a spot on the end of the bench closest to the cell door and draped himself with the pretense of innocence. His fellow prisoners took up stations facing the walls, minding their own business, except for Door, who was curled up on the floor like a shit beetle, moaning and sucking his knuckles. Jack sat with the toes of his high tops between the front bars, his back to the cell, eyes on the floor, but ready for whatever came next.

"Jackson Jude Bell?" A soft voice came from right in front of him. He looked up into the face of a tiny black woman, her hair a tight cap on her head, round, black eyes that reflected no light, and a mouth set in a firm "Don't give me no shit" line. Three guards loomed behind her, batons at the ready, glaring at the riffraff within, daring someone to make a move. Door groaned.

The tiny woman's importance and wordless demand for respect were instantly evident to Jack. Reminded of the nuns, he stood at attention, towering over her by a foot. "Yes, Ma'am."

She stepped back from the cell door without another word. A guard keyed it open, gesturing Jack out impatiently. With his middle finger behind his neck, Jack saluted the remaining company as the door clanged shut behind him and the guard led them upstairs.

The interview room was occupied, so they sat in chairs on opposite sides of the hallway studying each other. Jack was tired, hungry, and dirty, but most of all he was preoccupied with keeping this jam off Murph's radar. The old man had enough to worry about without having to drive into the city to throw Jack's bail, even though Jack knew that he could count on Murph if it came to that. *Ain't that what everyone wants? Someone to back our play?*

From inside his head, he heard a soft female voice say, *'Yes, Jack.'* He looked up and caught the tiny woman eyeing him closely. A half-smile crept across her face, but she quickly suppressed it.

"Ma'am?" he said aloud, unsure of himself for the first time that rocky day.

She looked at him intently for another half minute then stepped up to the guard who had to bend over from a great height so she could speak into his ear. He looked at Jack doubtfully and gestured for him to get up and follow them. Something had changed.

A flight of stairs and a short hallway later, they stopped at a frosted glass door, "Judge Avery X. O'Connor" on it in flaking gold letters. She tapped twice on the glass and opened the door without waiting to be admitted. Jack was right on her heels as a lean, older man looked up from a sheaf of papers in his right hand, his left working behind the ears of a small gray terrier curled in his lap.

"How's Max doing today?" she asked softly.

The Judge looked down at the dog. "Not so great. I think his time may come sooner than I'd hoped."

She handed him Jack's paperwork." I think you might be interested in this case." She watched the man's eyes as he took in Jack with one glance.

"What's the charge?"

"Fare beating on the Hudson. Possession, marijuana."

"Any evidence?"

She handed him a fat manila envelope.

The Judge glanced at the signatures on the outside and looked inside the envelope briefly, then slipped it into a desk drawer, all the while holding the paperwork up to hide a smile. *What wouldn't the fates do to put them in his sights?* He was grateful that the crime was so petty. It made erasing the paper trail much easier.

"Thank you, Violet. And you, take a seat." He pointed a meaty forefinger at Jack then crooked it toward one of two armchairs facing his desk. "You have no idea how lucky you are this morning." He didn't know if this encounter was serendipity or another example of his long-time clerk's tireless mission to find others like themselves. Other 'readers' or 'talents' or whatever Violet was calling them this week. He didn't have the energy for it anymore.

IT WAS wild chance that Violet had seen Jack's full name on the docket that morning. She knew she had to follow through. When she was still a social worker, she used to stop by Holy Spirit and visit with the nuns and the staff. She was there the day after an unknown teenager gave birth to a baby boy on the floor of the coat closet in the sanctuary vestibule. The baby lived, the mother didn't.

She'd hastily scribbled "Holy Spirit, boy unk" on the tab of a manila folder. With no other option for placing a newborn that day, it was her easy decision that left Jack in the care of the housekeeper and the sisters until something more satisfactory turned up. It never did.

A few weeks later, Violet came in off the hot city streets into the cool darkness of the motherhouse. Mother Briganda would be in the parlor in her rocking chair as she had daily for several years, robbed of her speech, and most of her sense, by a stroke. Violet still shivered at the memory. She'd stepped into the parlor to acknowledge the old woman, see if she needed anything. The baby had been tied securely into a makeshift sling across the old nun's lap. No one had heard a peep out of Briganda for years. Now, she was crooning softly, a lullaby in a language Violet didn't recognize.

The baby was awake, his round, solemn eyes fixed on the singer's face, one arm freed from the swaddling cloth. His little hand opened and closed like he was trying to catch the beam of sunlight that filtered down through a row of filthy glass panes set high in the front wall. The bar of light bathed the old nun and the newborn, Mother Briganda stopped singing and spoke to the baby, her voice clear.

"Never tell, Jack. Never let them know what you do." She dropped her voice to a whisper. "They won't hurt you. They'll hurt the ones you love. Come for them in the night." She leaned over and peered into the child's bright eyes. "Never tell. And if you can help it, never love."

Frozen in the doorway, the skin all over Violet's body prickled. Briganda turned in her rocker, smiled sadly, and said, "This one could change the world. If he lives."

Frightened, Violet shrank into the darkness of the hall and the old woman resumed her rocking and crooning. The child closed his eyes. Mother Briganda never uttered another word the remainder of her days. The light in the room was not all from the afternoon sun.

JACK HAD BEEN off Violet's radar since the Church abruptly transferred him to Graymoor when he was ten. She was excited to see what had become of him, but worried and anxious to have found him in police custody. *What had he been up to?* She'd stopped asking about him at the convent. There seemed no point since all anyone would tell her was that he got good grades. There had been rumors. If what she suspected was true, that Jack was a talent, of course he got good grades. If anyone in the room knew the answer to a question, so did Jack. He read anything and everything only to entertain himself. A charmer when he needed to be, he'd also been a rebellious troublemaker and instigator in school.

After the brief instant of contact she'd made with Jack in the corridor, he'd walled himself off from her and the judge and was a cipher. She was at a loss as to who or what they were dealing with.

JACK FELT the pall of the situation begin to lift a little, but he was puzzled by his inability to read either of them. The woman was a stone wall, and the judge felt wrapped in cotton the same color as the dog in his lap. Jack was in the dark about them and what might be next. Off-balance, but on guard.

On any other day, at this proximity, Jack would know them both through and through. Whatever was first on their minds would be his to use. It was not intuition. He'd move in close, just out of reach, look away, and know exactly what someone was thinking, but more importantly, what they would choose to do next given all the options they thought they had. He was rarely wrong.

He lumped people into three groups: Whites, Grays, and Voids. For the most part, people were Grays—consumed by themselves and their daily needs and pursuits. They were predictable, boring, and easily manipulated.

The Whites were the uncommon ones who spent their time concerned with the welfare of others. They were genuine; the anonymous donors, not the hymn singing hypocrites who spent most of their time patting themselves on the back hoping for media exposure.

And then there were the Voids. Blessedly rare, they spanned the spectrum of evil from just plain mean to the darkest hearts who killed without compunction. Jack could pick these out of a crowd and understood that somehow it was on him to keep tabs on them and move others out of harm's way if he could.

He was only ten when he canceled his first Void, the next when he was still a freshman in high school. Both killings were necessary, and he did what was expedient without a shred of self-doubt or guilt. But lately, taking care of business was getting in the way of having a good time. Jack Bell—judge, jury, and executioner—would much rather hustle, get high, and chase pussy.

The people he killed were undeniably guilty of heinous crimes. Jack had the power to recognize the monsters, and it was clear that exterminating them might be his calling. A calling. Something the priests at Graymoor talked about all the time, although he was pretty sure that his brand of action was not what they meant. They wanted new priests, not assassins. He was almost certain neither Violet nor the judge knew about his calling, or he would still be downstairs in the cage with Door and Company.

THE JUDGE CUT RIGHT to the chase. "So. You're a mind reader. Big deal." He'd dealt with enough minor talents to know that Jack was feeling uncertain about his world right now given that the one skill he counted on seemed to have disappeared. Jack sat back in the chair and opened his mouth to lie. The judge stopped petting the dog and raised his giant hand. "Don't say anything. Let me give you a little advice." For once, Jack snapped his mouth shut and listened. The judge went on. "Get smart. If you are not in school, get enrolled somewhere, learn a trade. Stop using what you know to get over on people. It could get you killed."

Jack thought *Thanks for nothing,* and the judge nodded and said, "You're welcome. I'm going to drop all charges and expunge any records if you'll give me your word that you'll stay out of trouble." It wasn't a question, and he didn't wait for Jack to answer. "How old are you?"

"Seventeen. In two weeks," Jack replied, realizing this man could make or break his future.

"Old enough to serve your country. How do you feel about the Navy? I hear they could still use a few good men." Again, he didn't wait for Jack to answer. "I'm going to dismiss the charges on the condition that you stop serving yourself for a while, grow up some and learn to take orders. Fit in if that's possible. There'll be no record when you get out."

That got Jack's attention. He had no way of knowing that the judge would put him into the hands of old friends who, without knowing why, would stand back and keep tabs on him. They would let him make mistakes and fail if need be, but no harm would come to him, and he'd never leave dry land.

It would please Violet too. Avery looked over at her and smiled, but she didn't respond. She was intent on Jack. *She should have been somebody's mother.* There was too little light in the world to waste Jack's potential, whatever that may be. What he would do with his gift would be up to him.

The judge gently lifted the tired old dog from his lap and settled it into a basket on the floor.

Jack considered everything for a moment. Right now, he didn't have a whole lot to lose or leave behind. He was bored and getting careless and there was that problem with the counterfeit money still ongoing. Murph was worried about him, and he hated that. The old man and his wife had been good to him, put him up when he needed shelter. No questions asked.

The judge stood up and put out his hand. "So, do we have an understanding?"

Jack rose and looked at the great white paw that hovered over the blotter. They shook hands and the older man's face turned somber, his suspicions about the level of Jack's abilities confirmed by the contact. There was an element to Jack that Avery couldn't decipher, and it nagged at him. He could tell that Violet sensed it too. An extra dimension neither of them had yet experienced in another talent.

Avery's level of skill paled before Violet's, but in their research, it was the norm that female talents had a broader, deeper reach than men. It was much more than intuition. Violet could cut to the heart of a person and their deepest motivations. Avery could only get immediate truths. It had served him well enough in court all these years. No truly innocent man went to jail when Avery O'Connor was sitting on the bench. The guilty paid dearly. Now, on Jack's behalf, calls would be made, rules bent, and changes set in motion.

FROM THE DAY Jack had ridden away from boarding school in the back of Murph's delivery truck, they'd known he was just a visitor. Murph had made the weekly produce delivery to Graymoor and was thinking that he was going to have to start coming twice a week or buy a bigger truck, but either way, money was no object. They wanted fresh eggs and meat now too. That was fine. An alumnus paid monthly, in cash, so the income was none of the government's business. Murph knew the contract with O'Connor was good as long as he breathed. It was an honest living. Life was good.

At a stop sign, he glanced in the side mirror and saw the boy in the truck bed. He'd helped himself to an apple from one of the boxes yet to be delivered and was laying in the straw eating it, staring at the sky, not a care in the world. School was out for the summer for him.

"Better on the back porch than on the streets," Murph told Tam. As with most teen-aged boys, Jack was all about himself and his plans. He did chores for his keep, but he came and went, never settling into their lives on the farm. Tam only set a place for him when she saw him walk through the door. She fed stray cats and dogs too. Now, they sat together at the kitchen table, everyone feeling the coming change.

Murph donned his hated reading glasses and went through the sheaf of papers Jack had brought home from the judge's office. Places for both their signatures were circled in red ballpoint. He was unconcerned that no one had asked for proof that anyone was Jack's legal guardian.

"From what I can see here, it's not a bad deal. The Navy. Now that they've finished with that bullshit in Viet Nam, you'll probably never get your feet wet. I think you should take the offer. I was Merchant Marine. No regrets."

All Jack could think about was not getting sucked into the legal system. It was time to step away from the game for a while. Try on something, be someone new. He picked up the pen and said softly so Tam couldn't hear him, "What the fuck," and started signing his full name over the scrawled red ovals.

Their niece was due home from college for the weekend and he didn't want to be around to have to meet someone new and explain himself and his situation. Not long after he first met Murph, the old man and his wife had driven him to the train station and Jack had gotten a brief glimpse of a frumpy-looking girl embracing Tam on the platform as the same train pulled away carrying him into the city.

There were two pictures of the girl pinned to a dusty corkboard by the back door with takeout menus, ticket stubs, and outdated coupons. A fuzzy, group graduation picture cut from the local paper and one of her as a teenager, working at the kitchen table making pies with Tam, a lattice-topped pie the focal point of the shot.

The sunlight was harsh and most of the girl's face in deep shadow. On the too-bright side, a half-closed eye, long lashes, round cheek, and a thick braid over her shoulder were just out of focus, dreamlike. She was wearing an apron over a sweatshirt and was holding out a ball of dough in long graceful fingers tipped with vicious-looking fingernails. The picture looked like a painting by Vermeer, everything about it saying 'home'. He wondered what it would be like to belong the way she seemed to.

Two days after signing the papers, Murph drove Jack into the city, and they met with the judge. Papers were counter-signed and Murph took the boy directly to La Guardia bound for Great Lakes, Illinois, with not much more than the clothes on his back. Jack would not be seventeen until the week basic training began and it would be a month short of two years before the Navy threw up its hands and put Jack back onto the street, but not the streets he remembered.

His meeting with the attorney appointed for him by the JAG office was a typical example of Jack working his way out of a jam. The guy was a Grey, a commoner, mostly preoccupied with his own immediate needs and concerns, easy to read and work. The case against Jack was full of holes. Everyone in the bakery had tested positive for pot and other drugs; it was party central for the downtrodden. There was not enough direct evidence to charge Jack as the one responsible for putting pot in a batch of brownies that had been served in the officer's mess. From the day he agreed to the enlistment, he'd done an admirable job of keeping his head down and blending in. The boredom factor was his downfall and the brownie episode his final undoing. Favors from old friends stretched wide and deep, but the Navy was done with Jack.

IN THE CRAMPED, cluttered office, Jack sat across the desk from the junior officer sorting through a pile of documents —Jack's service records, a maze of countersigned misdirection in triplicate. It was a year and nine months since he'd been dragooned—more than enough time to plant, grow and hatch out a human.

If Lt. Pinch-face had his way, they would up the enlistment age to twenty-one. Teenagers were more trouble than they were worth in a peacetime military.

The room was silent except for the whispering paper. Jack looked past the man's hunched shoulder at nothing and opened his mind to the man's thoughts. *He met a guy in a bar last night, a boy from Iowa with black, curly hair and long legs. Shit! He's gay and he can hardly stand himself, poor bastard.* The lieutenant looked up from the papers and stared at Jack, his eyes narrowed, and brow furrowed over his momentary loss of focus.

He felt it. Go easy now. Straight-faced, Jack winked at him ever so slightly, less than a twitch, and then looked away with a deadpan, vacant expression. *You imagined that.* It didn't always work, but it was worth a try.

Frowning, the young lieutenant blinked once in confusion, shivered visibly, and quickly wrote a memo to his

secretary to type up the orders of separation. Without preju-
dice. He wanted nothing more than to shake off this uncom-
fortable feeling and be done with Jack who was not his type.
In three days, and without any further audience with the
brass, Jack was on a train for home—unsuitable, but honor-
ably discharged. He never missed a beat or looked back.

~O~

S1:E10

Ivan Grolov waited calmly for his passport. There was no reason for worry at Logan Customs and Immigration, either for himself or for the bored official who stamped his passport, looked past Ivan, and muttered, "Next, please."

Grolov was just another businessman from Moscow, although his business this trip was personal and tragic: retrieving the mortal remains of his younger brother, Dmitri. He'd already filled out the paperwork and paid cash to ship the body back to the U.S.S.R. If the body could be found, that was.

His other business Customs didn't need to know about. One week, no more, and he would be home to deal with the fallout of this small disaster. The task of bringing Dmitri home was proving to be difficult and expensive - financially and emotionally. His favorite sibling had been murdered gruesomely by a woman (of all the indignities) and his body adrift somewhere in the bureaucratic nightmare of the undocumented dead in an old, overcrowded American city. Ivan had to admit, it was worse in Russia. In some cities, the unclaimed dead were incinerated with the trash. Dmitri lay in cold storage for two weeks before finally going into the ground with the other nameless and hapless poor.

Ivan would have to track Leon down and convince the fool that he wouldn't kill him when he saw him. Leon hadn't even tried to claim the body. Pure cowardice, Ivan supposed, but it was just as well. No doubt he would have implicated himself in the other deaths. Idiots. Both of them.

Still, they were both his brothers. The body would be found, and the wheels of revenge set in motion. He would bring Leon back to the U.S.S.R. with him even if he had to drug him and put him in the box with Dmitri. Leaving Leon in the U.S. unattended was asking for trouble. Eventually, Dmitri's murderer would be tracked down and made to pay. Ivan still couldn't believe Leon's account of the killing. A woman?

Leon had called Ivan in the middle of the night, collect of course, and wasted ten minutes and God knows how much of his money, sobbing and gibbering unintelligibly, slipping back and forth between Russian and garbled English, before finally delivering the bad news.

"How does one forget one's mother tongue in three years?" Ivan muttered to himself. A soft, alcohol-sodden mind was how. He nearly hung up on Leon, thinking he was calling from the drunk tank again, asking for bail. Then the words 'Dmitrty ubityye' came through, and Ivan sat heavily in the chair by the phone-stand in the dark apartment. A great sob welled up from inside of him, and it was a long minute before he could compose himself enough to drag the necessary details out of Leon.

Ivan had raised his two younger brothers and pinned his hopes on Dmitri. All three of the Grolov men were handsome, which was not good for much without brains. Leon was the baby, and his mental shortcomings likely related to their mother's drinking while she carried him. When their mother finally died of a combination of grief and alcoholism, Ivan was saddled with his brothers, five and ten years younger than himself. Only eighteen at his mother's death, he put his plans for university aside and took up the quickest and easiest way to make a living—his father's trade —smuggling.

All the old man's business connections were in the black market and Ivan had no trouble making his way in the family business. He refused to traffic in anything as dangerous and imprudent as drugs. Who needed the aggravation? Grolov Import Export shipping containers went west with crates of stolen liquor and bootleg copies of VHS movies, eight-tracks, and cassette tapes, then returned with stolen cars, trucks, and electronics. The money poured in. He set Dmitri and Leon up in Boston to handle the stateside logistics and keep them out of trouble in Russia.

All Dmitri and Leon were required to do was manage the ever-increasing number of outlets—truck stops, and corner stores spread out between Logan and Newark airports. Each month his brothers drove a route between the locations, paying intermediaries, checking inventory, and collecting cash. There wasn't even any heavy lifting.

The problem was they had too much time on their hands. The two of them behaved like a couple of sailors on liberty. Too lazy to acquire the necessary social skills to date American women, they spent ridiculous amounts of money on prostitutes. Dmitri gambled and lost more than he won.

Leon was lucky he hadn't already been deported for stupid petty crimes like littering and public intoxication. Ivan was at the point of pulling the plug on both of them, but the business still brought in much more than they cost him, so far. And if they were home with him in Russia?

What then? Who knows what kind of problems they would cause him?

Then Ivan made the mistake of agreeing to a favor for a friend of one of his union connections in New York. Corrupt petty bureaucrats, the lot of them. Incompetents who would be eaten alive in his country. All the man wanted was someone to watch a young woman who was going to college in Boston and report back to him. How hard could that have been? His brothers were already in the city. He thought Dmitri might seize on this little extra responsibility as an opportunity for advancement. Leon, he had no hope for.

But Dmitri had been annoyed at more time-consuming busy work and dumped the new assignment on his younger brother without telling Ivan. He gave Leon a Polaroid picture of the girl.

"She's a real dumpling, Leon, just your type."

"What's her name?" Leon said, holding the photo two inches from his nose.

Dmitri cuffed him on the back of the head, "You don't need to know her name. You're only watching her." The address was on the back. So was her name.

Women intimidated Leon. He blushed and stuttered so badly that Dmitri would tell the girls they paid for that it was his first time, every time. Leon studied the photograph.

Dmitri warned him again. "Don't get close enough for her to identify you. Hang back. All the man wants to know is if she's seeing anyone, cheating on him. We don't need to know what she eats for breakfast. Don't fuck this up now; we need the extra money."

"How much money?" Leon fanned his face with the picture.

Dmitri swung at him and missed. He shouted, "Listen to you! I pay the rent, the utilities and what do you do? Drink and watch the fucking TV. You'll do this right, or I'll send you back to Ivan."

It wasn't hard work. Leon blended in well enough in a college town with his long hair, worn pea coat, and engineer boots. He found that the girl spent the most time at the public library in the reference section. Whole days sometimes. She sat at the same table near a window on the top floor, huge books spread open on the polished wood. Pictures of plants were everywhere. She sketched the plants and then made notes alongside the drawings.

Against Dmitri's warnings, he followed her inside and spent time wandering around as if he was looking for something. The girl dressed like a homeless person. Granted, the weather was raw and cold, but he had not yet seen her in a dress. Sweatshirts zipped up over sweaters, sweatpants, boots, scarves, mittens. Was he going to have to wait until summer to see what she really looked like? Despite a perpetually annoyed expression, she was beautiful.

Leon was good looking, blue eyes, thick, black hair long to his collar. He wore round, wire-rimmed glasses, "like Lennon", he'd told the optometrist. He was big—six-foot-one, 210 pounds, but soft and getting sloppy. He loathed exercise, any sport. He watched TV obsessively and went to the movies alone and wept in the dark.

Increasingly bored and frustrated with just watching the girl, he made a bold move that could have led to disaster. The library was busy. He followed her up the steps but detoured into the men's room where he sat in the stall and drank from the metal flask of vodka he carried more faithfully than his wallet. He washed his hands, splashed water into his bloodshot eyes, combed his hair, and practiced a smile and a nod in the smudged mirror.

He took the seat at the end of the same long table where

she worked. She didn't even look up at first. *Idiot!* Dmitri was right. In a building full of them, he hadn't even brought a damned book with him. He lifted a copy of the Boston Herald from the pile of dailies on the table and spread it open to the obituaries. He and Dmitri made a few good scores by going to poorly attended wakes, then breaking into the apartments of the dead during their funerals. He had a pen, but nothing to write on. He was sure the fates were speaking to him.

"Excuse me, please." He had been unable to shed his accent. "May I borrow, um, have a piece of paper?"

She looked up from her work, a detailed sketch of some kind of vine, focused wide gray eyes on him for a moment and, without reply, plucked a sheet of lined paper from the back of her notebook and slid it across the table to him.

Did she smile at him? Was that new color in her cheek? He almost bit his tongue choking off '*spasiba*' then stuttering, "Thank you." He forced himself to the task of copying names and addresses from the newspaper carefully avoiding the place where he'd seen her finger and thumb grip the page before she'd floated the paper and that smile his way. As much as he wanted to, he couldn't look at her again. Then, at once, she thrilled and terrified him. Without speaking, she bummed a drink from him. Her mouth to his flask was almost more than he could bear.

With shaking hands, he folded the piece of paper and slipped it into his pocket under the empty flask. His holy relic. Had she seen him rubbing his finger over that spot on the paper? In a panic, he got up and fled. The girl never looked up from her work and he never went back inside the library.

.   .   .

THE FOLLOWING DAY, Leon started watching her through a hunting scope from the roof of a building nearby, trading his obsession for the movies with one for 'Ahna'.

One of the girls in the apartment never seemed to wear clothes. He saw the blonde naked so often he was bored with her skinny, whoring ass. The others were nurses—they spent most of their time in scrubs unless they were dressing to go out on dates.

Anna never joined them. He sighed and put the scope down on the blanket beside him. He lay on his back and looked up into the featureless night. He felt sorry for her. She had less life than he did. He lit a joint and rolled back onto his stomach and resumed his vigil just in time to see the other girls come down the front steps and get into a car. Anna was alone. He was ready to call it a night when a light came on in a room on the top floor of her building. The high-powered scope let him see remarkable detail.

It had been a sunny day, and the curtains were wide open. Small plants in tiny paper cups lined the deep windowsill. He watched as she undressed, not quite believing his luck as each garment fell away. Dmitri had called her a dumpling, a reference to the fact that Leon preferred girls with big tits and asses. To Leon, Anna was perfect.

Naked, except for socks, she twisted her thick hair on top of her head and wandered around the room until she came back to the windowsill, found a hair clip, and started watering the plants. Oh God, how he loved plants now. Her big, round breasts defied gravity. The apartment must have been warm. Her nipples were spread softly, tan with dark pink tips. He opened his mouth wide as if to suckle and rocked his erection side to side, grinding into the sleeping bag beneath him.

She bent to pick something up from the floor and disappeared from view leaving him bereft. Then she moved back into his line of sight again and he almost fainted. She was down on all fours looking for something under a piece of furniture. She groped under the chair, her arm extended, and cheek pressed to the floor, the position putting her ass in the air, her knees apart. The slash of her sex filled the lens and Leon reached out with one hand to touch her and came before he could unzip his jeans.

She got to her feet and left the room, flicking off the light as she went. He collapsed face down on the sleeping bag. He was up on the roof every night for the next ten days, rain or shine, but she never repeated the performance. The plants flourished, and he stopped talking about her to Dmitri giving only the shortest of answers when asked about her activity. The last thing he wanted to do was share Anna with his brother.

Of course, Dmitri was wise to his brother's infatuation. Suspicious of Leon's sudden feigned indifference to the girl, he started watching Anna himself, sometimes shadowing Leon who was comically oblivious.

One evening, while Leon lost himself in a cheap movie theater and a pint of vodka, Dmitri followed her into a shop Leon had never mentioned. Occult Books and Supplies. Witches and other bullshit. He went in and browsed books about spiritualism and native wisdom, sniffed at all the candles and incense, and fingered the crystals as he watched her clients come and go. He even asked the old man at the register about her hours and rates. *Fucking hippies!*

DMITRI HAD three rolls of quarters ready when he called Ivan from a payphone in the park. Paying for this call himself mattered. He shivered with the anticipation of his big brother's approval. Of course, he'd paid no attention to the time differences and woke Ivan up.

"Ivan, did your friend in New York tell you why he wants this woman watched?"

Groggily, Ivan said, "He told me they will be married when she tires of this college nonsense and comes home. All he wants to know is if she is being faithful to him. The fool."

"Do you believe that?"

"He's an arrogant idiot, but he pays me every month like clockwork, and I pay you. Why should I care what she really does? Tell me!"

"Ivan, she's a witch. A fortune-teller. The cards, Ivan, she can see the future. She gives readings at a shop. I've watched her customers' faces when they leave her. They always come back, week after week." Seconds of transatlantic silence ticked by and the operator demanded another twenty quarters. Dmitri cursed the entire time he plugged the coins into the box.

"Ivan. Are you there?"

"Yes, Dmitri. Are you sure?"

"Yes. I'm taking her, Ivan. We can use her."

"The risks?

"None. She's only a woman. You'll see."

LEON SNORED like a bulldozer when he was drunk. He was a six-pack into *General Hospital* when he nodded off, the color Polaroid of Anna on his thigh. Her head and shoulders in profile, streaked blond hair blowing around her, as much of a smile as he had yet seen on her. Her eyes squinted at something distant, the curve of her cheek cut off by a red scarf.

Dmitri pulled the photo out from under his brother's sweaty palm and glared at it. He kicked the ottoman out from under Leon's feet making him grunt and open his bleary eyes wide.

"What have you done?" Dmitri shook the photo in his brother's face.

"What do you mean?" Leon reached to snatch it away from him and failed.

"Did you talk to her; have you been bothering her?"

"No, no nothing like that. I just watch her, like you said."

"This is my own fault. I should have known you'd fall for this cow." Dmitri slapped him open-handed. "Did you speak to her?"

Leon cringed; his hands held over his head. "No!" It wasn't quite a lie, "and she's not a cow." He was crying.

"All I asked you to do was watch her. See if she was seeing anyone," Dmitri shouted. He didn't mention that he'd been watching Leon following her like a stray dog, then spending hours a day watching her himself. Discovering the shop where she gave Tarot readings.

"She's alone, I tell you." Leon whimpered.

"For your sake you better be right. I'm sick of running Ivan's business for him. The man in New York has offered me a job there. I can get out from under big brother." Lying to Leon was easiest. Best

"You can't leave me here." Leon was panicky.

"I will if you've tipped this woman off. Shut up. Stop crying before I smash your face in. I'm going to show you just what women are good for. Solve the man's problem for him and put an end to this nonsense so we can get out of this shit-hole city."

Leon was afraid to ask what he meant and eyed the clock anxiously. He was running out of time. She would be at the library in her usual place, and today he was determined to speak to her. Warn her, but he didn't get the chance. Dmitri said, "Go get cleaned up. I'm going to need you to drive."

"RIGHT THERE AT the end of the block. A parking space. Hurry, idiot. Keep your eyes on the door."

Dmitri slapped at the buttons over the tarnished mailboxes, and someone buzzed him in without asking who it was. He had been repeating the word "pizza" over and over and was shocked when the door lock clicked open with no challenge. He slipped inside and hid behind the inner door of the small lobby. One of the nurses was coming down the stairs. There could be no witnesses.

Karen died instantly. He stepped from behind the door and slashed at the back of her head; the blade catching her at the base of her skull, the cash for the pizza fluttering to the floor. She collapsed in a heap at his feet, and he stepped over her body, careful to avoid the pool of blood that spread quickly across the floor.

He took the steps two at a time almost crashing into Netty as she came out of the communal bathroom with a towel wrapped around her hips, bare breasts still damp. She stared at him in shock and moved to cover herself, but he grabbed her by the face with one gloved hand, pushing her hard against the door.

There was no expression on his face, no life in his eyes as he subdued her flailing with his whole body.

"Anna?"

Netty tried to shake her head from side to side to make him understand that Anna was not there, but she had seen

Karen's body and the killer's face. He kissed her roughly and drove the tip of the blade through her heart, clean through to the door.

Inside the apartment, Maryann lay face-down on her bed, an empty bottle of wine on the floor and a half-filled glass on the nightstand. She was naked, a sheet just covering her hips and legs and he stood there watching her a long minute, touching himself through his clothing. She shifted position in her sleep, turning her face to the wall, the sheet slipping, exposing her buttocks. He put the knife on the floor next to the wine bottle and pulled the sheet off her completely and still she didn't move.

He fell on her, stifling her screams with his hand as he raped her. She stopped struggling, perhaps in hope that he would come quickly and not hurt her, but he dropped his full weight on her making it even more difficult for her to breathe. His coarse cheek scraped hers as he rasped in her ear, "Where's Anna?" then took his hand away from her mouth.

She screamed again, and he pressed her face into the pillow, reached down for the knife, and drove it through her until he felt the resistance of the mattress and she bucked under him once, a violent spasm. It felt good; her fighting that way, and he was sorry he had wasted the others.

He stabbed her again, but this time there was no fight and his thoughts returned to Anna. All these weeks of watching her, his half-baked plan of taking her had come to this fuck up. He was so swamped with self-pity and rage he didn't hear her until it was too late.

~O~

The last time Anna saw Ray before she left for Boston was the first time she saw Sam.

Ray had let her come with him to score an ounce of pot. The run-down mansion was high on the ridge between the post road and the reservoir and had a reputation for a place you didn't want to be when you heard sirens. He said the weed was a going-away present for her, but she knew he was scoping out the place with an eye toward buying it out from under the current owners for little more than back taxes. He'd warned her to stay in the car while he went inside.

A quartet of motorcycles blocked anyone from parking near the front entrance and a half dozen ripely overflowing garbage cans flanked it. The place was occupied by an ever-changing collection of derelicts and petty criminals. No signs of life anywhere except for distant, muffled rock music and the smell of burnt meat. Unannounced visits by the cops were a regular thing, and Ray was nervous and cranky.

Bored, Anna defied Ray one more time and got out of the car to check out the grounds. The front door was open. Through the trash-strewn lobby and the open rear door, she could see the neglected lawn bounded by a stone wall behind the building and in the distance, a sparkling body of water.

Hot, sweaty, and a little lost, she picked her way through the scrubby trees beyond the wall, trying to find a path down to the reservoir, cursing out loud as she went. As she looked for the horizon to get her bearings, the air in front of her shimmered and she thought she was getting a migraine. She squeezed her eyes shut tight, deepened, and slowed her breathing, trying to fend it off.

A cool breeze washed over her, pushing back the nausea. She took a few deep breaths, relaxed, and opened her eyes to a benign presence. A young man stood right in front of her—solid as flesh, sweet as honey, his long, sandy hair fluttering in that breeze, the sun lighting his smile and sparkling out of his blue eyes.

Her strident "Where the fuck is the trail?" had shocked Sam, but with no useful answers for her, he smiled and held out his hand as if asking her to dance. Without thinking, Anna took his hand and their energies overlapped for a few flickering moments before he was gone like a soap bubble popping on the wind.

In those few seconds, Anna came to know Samuel Archer Fortune cradle to grave—who he was, how he lived and hoped, and, sadly, how he died. Caught off-guard by the sudden contact and rush of Sam's energy and emotions, she put her hands over her face and sobbed. *What do they want from me?*

It wasn't the first time Anna communed with the dead, but it hadn't happened since she was a young child. Back then, she'd accepted such things as ordinary. Ghosts were no more or less than memories made manifest. Now, her heart squeezed up into her throat. Desperate to get high, she abandoned her search for the way down to the water and hurried back to Ray's car.

WHEN SHE ARRIVED in Boston with only a month's supply, Anna's first order of business was getting the pills she needed to function. She didn't know what to expect, wanted only to be ready for the worst—thousands of displaced, unhappy, immature men and women in close proximity, under constant pressure. There was no safe way to make a doctor understand what she needed and why. Their family doctor, Bernie Cohen, knew only that she suffered from what he called "situational anxiety," but she wouldn't ask him, afraid that it would get back to Tam and Murph. Without those mother's little helpers, she'd wind up committed before the first semester was over.

She lined up three appointments with three different low-rent GPs on the same day. All she needed to do was sit in the chair at the office or clinic, sigh from the bottom of her soul, and let her eyes fill with tears while she spoke of sleeplessness and anxiety and told the good doctors how hard it was for her to be away from home for the first time. They usually started writing before the first teardrop fell. How easily those tears came! The rainbow selection of drugs she scored would keep her safe from the shitstorm of the emotional blowback swirling around college life. What-ever she didn't use, she'd easily trade for pot.

That done, she lined up Tarot clients through a bulletin board at a nearby occult bookstore. A loan and a scholar-ship took care of tuition, the rest would be on her. From the beginning, she charged twice the going rate for readings and the tactic worked, drawing in curious clients with more money than sense, and friends just like them. She'd go into a first meeting sober, suffer whatever the client was obsessing over, and give a reading with just enough star quality to hook them. By the end of the first semester, she had enough regular clients and a steady income, but she booked readings deep into the night and there were days when she could barely get out of bed for classes without chemical bolstering. Between the whites, blacks, yellows, and blues, balance was slipping through her fingers.

Days on campus unfolded in a monotonous blur. Studying was the excuse she used to avoid the pressures of blending into a whole new social order. She had no intention of fitting in, making friends or partying. Juggling a heavy course load and Tarot clients kept her from having to think too much about the point of it all. Going away to college had just seemed like the next logical step in her life, but deep down she knew that the escape she was looking for wouldn't happen in Boston or any other city.

From the time she could talk and Tam and Murph understood what she was capable of, they'd taught her she was different and that she had to keep that difference a secret. *Never tell. Never let on.* It was a game until she was old enough to understand how dire the consequences might be if the wrong people knew what she could do. Going away to college hadn't changed any of that.

Moving out of the dorm helped. It gave her perverse satisfaction to take money from Ray. He'd insisted on giving her enough to find a place off-campus. He hadn't even seen her off when she left home, but she hadn't been gone a week when he started calling, playing the forlorn boyfriend. She hoped that sharing an apartment would keep him from thinking he could come up anytime he wanted. From a notice posted on a bulletin board, she found a place with three female students. They had a whole floor of a tired brownstone owned by absentee landlords. Anna took what was left; the tiny room was little more than a closet. She bought a single bed.

To her embarrassed annoyance, Ray still dropped by unannounced. He would arrive all road-weary and pathetic and offer to take her out to dinner. All he ever wanted to talk about was her quitting school and coming home. He'd bought an apartment house and was getting a salary from the union. He needed her help to stay on top of all his business contacts. Give him a desperately needed advantage. Whenever he showed up, she made of point of taking enough pills to keep herself cut off from his selfish arrogance. It was always all about Ray. She let him ramble on until they were well into their entrees before she let him have it. "I know what you want Ray and I'm not going to do it anymore. I have a life here."

"This?" he gestured broadly as if the overpriced surf and turf restaurant represented her entire existence. "This is a joke. And organic chemistry? Gimme a break. What do you think you're going to do with a degree in making LSD or whatever the fuck?"

Anna had to press her lips together to keep from mouthing his words. She didn't even bother to tell him she didn't need his money anymore. Instead, she let him grind on about supporting her as she sipped her wine and sank further into a cottony apathy. Her lack of response, her unwillingness to rise to a fight was making him desperate.

He shut up abruptly and stared at her, leaning to one side in his chair to see what she was wearing. "You're seeing someone, is that what it is?" Without waiting for a denial, he reached across the table and grabbed her wrist, her fork still poised in her hand. "If you're cheating on me..."

She didn't flinch or resist but leaned his way. "If I was

cheating on you Ray, I would have let you come back to my place and watch how a real man takes care of a woman. Get the waiter. I changed my mind about dessert."

He dropped her arm like he'd been scalded. He ripped off his napkin, banged it down on the table noisily and stormed out of the restaurant, once again sticking her with the check. Each time she would linger over dessert and tip handsomely.

Four times in six weeks the ugly dance repeated. Then she got an unsigned postcard that he'd taken the trouble to print. As long as they had been together, he'd never used the word *love*, but between the *when* and the *ever* he'd crammed a scrawny heart that looked more like a fang with rotted roots. The visits ended.

"Ms. Catalano, are you sure you're in the right class?"

Amber-tinted aviator sunglasses gave her an air of disconnection and, rather than take notes in class, she sketched. Detailed, almost photographic likenesses of the teachers, other students, whatever was in her line of sight. Her history professor grew annoyed when she refused to engage with him. Anna looked at the sketch she'd been working on during his lecture. She tilted it so he could see it easily.

"Is this you, Dr. Becker?" Like most of her professors, he was a self-absorbed bore.

"Yes, it's a good likeness, but..."

"Then, I'm in the right place." Despite appearances, Anna's grades attested to the fact that she was paying full attention. By the middle of her sophomore year, a place on the dean's list would have been a lock, except for the notes that started turning up in her mailbox.

When she wasn't in class or in the library, Anna was in her room or out on the fire escape or the roof, anywhere to be alone. There was nothing homey about her place, no communal meals or activities. Karen and Netty were nursing students with hellish schedules. Maryann was the house problem child—their resident party animal—the one who had enough drama for all of them. She was beautiful but attracted the worst sort of men, one user after the next.

The last time Ray dropped by unannounced, he was with a guy who quickly became Maryann's latest. While Ray fumed and left because Anna wasn't home, his friend stuck around. Dmitri was good-looking enough if you liked rough trade, but he barely spoke English. Maryann laughed. "I didn't let him stay for the conversation."

ANNA FELT LIKE SHIT. Was it the moon? She hated to admit that, like all women, she was at the mercy of the tides of her body. *Or was it the drugs?* She took what she needed when she needed it, and the temptation to dig a Valium hole and pull the edges tight around her was strong. The line between normal and drooling idiot was becoming precarious.

Maybe she was getting the flu. *What day was it?* She thought again about taking the prescription bottle out of her bag and checking the contents, making calculations. The five-milligram bubble that usually carried her through lunch was more like a tattered plastic construction fence—wisps and snatches of other people's thoughts and emotions hitting her like large, hairy moths from the moment she opened her eyes. She was exhausted from flinching. On top of all of it all, she woke up in a shroud of soul-crushing loneliness.

She thought about the mechanics of getting to her next class on time and decided it was out of the question. What she needed was to put herself on the disabled list for a few days. Go to bed sober, sleep hard, eat right, and try to pull herself together.

Anna hadn't gone home for the February break, in fact, she hadn't even told anyone there was one. In their last phone conversation, Murph mentioned that they were letting some runaway boy stay with them—sleeping in her old bed, even—and she was fine with it. Someone for Tam to cook for and fuss over. She didn't like to think about them missing her.

She went to the movies alone, but the films she gravitated to just made matters worse. It was after eleven when Anna got home. Karen, Netty, and Maryann were in the kitchen laughing and talking. Maryann had just kicked the new guy out. His bossiness and hot temper had gotten on her nerves for the last time. Karen and Netty were making fun of her.

"He was a good lay, but I couldn't make him understand when enough was enough. He was generous. Got to give him that." She held out her arm so they could all see the trinket. "Look at this!" It was one of those gold Tiffany cuff bracelets that had to be put on with a screwdriver.

Netty spun the trinket on Maryann's wrist and said, "Betcha it's hot."

Maryann said, "That should matter how?" They all laughed. Karen brayed like a donkey. They sat together around the table and dragged Dmitri over the coals.

"Are you going to give it back?"

"And sell myself cheap?" Maryann leaned on one elbow and smoked while the other two worked on removing the bracelet with a butter knife. Dmitri had kept the tiny screwdriver it came with. "Don't think so. Pawnshop here I come."

It was the laughter that caught Anna by surprise, bringing on a fresh round of stifled tears. Laughing together with friends, the feeling of being with people who you can be yourself with, trust, were things she would never have in her life. Overwhelmed with homesickness and the knowledge that she faced a lifetime of being cut off from these ordinary pleasures, she went up the fire escape to smoke a joint and look for stars that wouldn't come out. Waking up there at dawn when a pigeon shit hot and wet in the palm of her hand should have been deeply disturbing, but for Anna, it was just another new, lonely day.

ANNA SHOOK herself out of the extended, fruitless reverie and went back to the sketch she started an hour earlier. It was ruined. Fat teardrops marred a section of cross-hatching intended to give depth and definition to a cluster of leaves. The ink had blurred into dark clouds and ran a muddy track down the page.

Choose how now. She heard Tam's voice in her heart. Break and cry for real or take a breath and start fresh. She breathed deep and an acrid whiff of vodka caught her by surprise.

When she wasn't paying attention, a man had taken the chair at the end of her table. He took up a shocking amount of space. How had she not seen him approach? He was over six feet tall. Elvis if he was trying to be a Beat poet. Pale complected, long, black hair to his collar. Brutally handsome, but shabby looking, overdue for a shower and shave. He took off round, green sunglasses to reveal intense, blue eyes shaded by sweeps of lashes that were so long, on a woman you'd know they were fake. He was wrapped blissfully in a cloud of alcohol. Anna wished more people drank and took drugs. She was selfishly grateful for whatever misery put him in the bag at ten in the morning.

He opened a newspaper to the back. The classified section? *A jobseeker? Apartment hunter?* He groped a pen from an inner pocket of his pea-jacket as he looked around like he'd misplaced something. The top of a metal flask glinted in the weak sunlight that washed across the table. He looked over at her and stammered, "May I borrow, um, have a piece of your paper?" A foreign accent. She pulled a sheet of lined paper from her notebook and slid it across the polished wood to him. Shyly, he stuttered, "*Spasiba*" She nodded once and turned back to her work.

Holding the sketch pad on her lap, she turned to a fresh page and began sketching him as he bent to some task, his arm curled around the paper the way left-handers will, frowning in concentration. Line by line, Leon Grolov came to life under her pen. The strong line of his nose, the sweep of dirty hair, those lush lashes, his jaw knotted over some frustration.

After a few minutes, she reached out and patted the table to get his attention, then tipped her hand as if pouring a drink and lifted her chin, letting him know she's seen the flask in his coat. She held her hand up and flicked three fingers back to herself in the universal gesture of "gimme".

He blinked at her and wet his lips. She copied that gesture deliberately and added half a smile. He looked around furtively and passed her the aluminum canteen, watching intently as she took two full swallows, gasped at the rush, and wiped her mouth on the back of her hand. She screwed the cap on and passed it back to him. They nodded at each other solemnly.

She turned back to the drawing, and with a few more strokes, captured Leon's likeness as surely as the Polaroid in his shirt pocket had captured hers. As quickly as he had arrived, he got up and walked away without a word or backward glance.

ANNA DIDN'T KNOW she was being stalked until she found the second note left in her mailbox at the student center. "Meet me outside at 10" was first. She blew it off as a mistake. The boxes had no names, only numbers. It was probably meant for someone else. *Outside where? And did they mean am or pm? Jerk.* She crumpled it up and threw it away without another thought.

Two days later, there was a second note hastily printed by the same hand on a piece of white paper torn from a food delivery bag. This one chilled her. She stuffed it into her bag and went to the library where she sat at her table, took the crumpled note out of her bag and smoothed it out.

In blocky print, 'Dont ignore me Anna! Clayborns tomorrow 830'. He knew her name, and the tone was a command, not a request. *Fuck you, Charlie!* Angry more than frightened, she balled up the note and threw it in the trash. Fear would have been a good thing, but she couldn't get past the creepiness of someone invading her privacy. Danger never figured in.

The next day a man followed her from the library back to the brownstone. He was taking unnecessary chances, following her this way, but what started out as just a paying job had quickly become an obsession.

Anna was on the roof smoking a joint watching a couple on the roof of the next building argue. She couldn't hear what was being said over the rock music that was pounding out of the open third-floor windows, but the body language was perfectly clear. He was accusing her of something, and she was refusing to own up to whatever it was.

Anna's buzz was leveling out when she felt a wave of unease and nausea that began building like layers of sound that no one else could hear. She'd been chilled in the night air but was suddenly drenched with sweat. She went back down the fire escape and ducked through the kitchen window and called out.

"Hello, is anyone here?" No one had seen her slip out the window earlier. Anna opened the hall door and fell over Netty's naked body painted with blood from a great gash in her chest. It looked as if someone had ripped out her heart.

Frozen in shock, the pleasant high yanked out from under her like a cruel magician's tablecloth, Anna forced her eyes away from Netty and looked down the stairs to where Karen lay in a huge pool of blood, her head angled grotesquely away from her body. With no idea whether the killer had fled, Anna stumbled back into the apartment, locked the door, and leaned against it, rigid with fear. Eyes squeezed shut, willing calm, she called into the void for help with no real hope of an answer. Death was at hand.

Slipping from the shadows unseen, Sam Fortune shimmered and wrapped Anna in a protective darkness, a cold embrace. Something fierce gripped her heart—a flare of pain that just as quickly shrank to a hot glow at her core. The world around her slowed, sounds retreated. Power flowed into her body. It was not a matter of courage.

She moved from the front door to the first bedroom and watched the man fumbling his pants up over his bare ass as he loomed over Maryann's nude body. Time had ceased to be a concern for Karen, Netty, and Maryann. Everyone she knew always seemed to be racing towards something. Not for them. Not anymore for the killer and not for herself. She had all the time in the world. The room seemed to shrink, and the air went as cold and dry as a meat locker. She could see her breath.

He might have sensed Anna standing behind him because he leaned over and reached for the weapon on the floor. More a sword than a knife, it was two feet long, a third of that, the leather-wrapped handle. The double-edged blade was glazed with blood. It looked heavy, cumbersome, and crude.

She watched a fat drop of Maryann's blood fall from his hand to splash brightly on the pale rag rug above the tip of the blade, like the dot of an "i". His bloodstained hand was floating down to the knife when her hand slipped into the shadow of his and took it the way the gulls at the beach steal a sandwich even as you lift it to your mouth.

His hand closed on nothing, and she heard a sub-aural grunt as he looked down to where the knife had been.

Anna placed one knee on the bed and gripped the weapon like a Louisville slugger. Left-handed, like the great Ted Williams, she swung for the fences, her fluid follow-through ending in a bone-jarring stop as the tip of the blade bit deep into the plaster wall and stuck there.

Severed just above a prominent Adam's apple, Dmitri's head bounced off the wall and landed face up, encircled in the crook of Maryann's arm, her fingers clawed deep into her pillow in death. Anna watched his face as he seemed to watch his own headless body rise to its knees, stall like a stunt plane at the top of a too steep loop and topple off the bed heavily. The mouth went slack, and the blue eyes drifted to a point over her shoulder and stayed open.

Anna caught a flicker of movement beyond the window on the fire escape. The inside of the window had a rime of melting frost. What she had first thought was a pale face, was only her own reflection.

It wasn't fair, his lack of suffering.

SAM WEPT as he released her. His frozen tears bloomed as brief spots of frost on her hands and in her hair and were gone as quickly as they appeared. He hovered beside her in the kitchen as she dialed O from the wall phone and sat down to wait, his grim energy the only thing keeping her conscious.

The killer's blood had fountained from his neck spattering everything, and she was misted with it. Shivering violently with the sudden cold of the room, the heat of pain flared in her arm and shoulder, pulling her back into the terrible moment. Alone.

By the time the police got there, she'd drifted into a safe, unreachable place, only able to tell them she couldn't remember anything from the time she saw the girls dead. She wished it were true and tried to believe it. The cops did. By the time paramedics arrived, she'd allowed herself to spiral back to the panic and reacted violently to their attempts to examine her, screaming when they touched her. In the struggle, she threw herself back in the chair, hitting her head on the wall hard enough to knock herself unconscious.

~O~

S1:E12

L eon had left his gloves in the car and teetered on the steps of the fire escape; his hands jammed in his pockets. *What was taking so long? Where was he?*

The skinny girl was asleep on the bed. A bedside lamp cast a dim, pink glow over her naked back leaving her head in darkness. There was no sound from inside. Beyond the bed, Dmitri's silhouette filled the doorway.

LEON WATCHED as his brother crept to the foot of the bed and looked out the window right at him. He watched as Dmitri fell on the girl, choking her, thrusting himself into her. Watching the struggle made Leon hard against his will and he was sick to his stomach.

Annoyed with her thrashing and noise, Dimitri brutally punched the long blade through her twice then dropped it to the floor. She stopped moving, and he went right on fucking her. Leon was furious with him. None of this was necessary. His dismay turned to terror as he saw Anna come up behind his brother who was too busy screwing a corpse to notice he wasn't alone.

She looked Russian, still dressed for the cold; a sweater, jeans, and boots, her hair pulled back into a thick braid. Every time Leon saw her heart-shaped face, her eyes the color of stone, he felt homesick. He willed her to look up, see past the horror on the bed. He was bewitched, overwhelmed by his well-worn memory of her naked body, but he couldn't remember her ever showing any kind of emotion. Now she appeared intent, a glimmer of something terrifying in those wide eyes and an almost smile.

Frozen with fear and indecision, he did nothing even as Dmitri finally sensed her approach. Leon opened his mouth to shout a warning but choked on his own saliva and clutched the iron railing desperately.

In a smooth, almost balletic move, she stole the blade from under Dmitri's hand and swung it in a mighty arc that severed his head cleanly from his body. It bounced off the wall and dropped onto the pillow beside the dead girl, face up. Blood sprayed everywhere and Dmitri toppled heavily onto the dead girl then slumped to the floor. Anna lifted her head and stared out the window into the dark through a blaze of frost that had formed in swirls on the inside of the glass.

A cold, wet pressure surrounded Leon as if he had fallen through thin ice and had no adrenaline to save himself. He recoiled into deeper shadows and almost fell from the metal stairs. From the darkness, he watched her get up from the bed and, without a backward glance at the carnage, go into the room beyond, use the phone on the wall very briefly, then drop into a nearby chair, the receiver still in her hand forgotten. He loved her and look what she'd done!

Leon had watched his brother die. He'd let it happen. He

might have interfered, distracted her, but he didn't and couldn't even ask himself why. Choking back vomit, he fled down the fire-escape in terror, mentally listing his defenses with each clattering flight. Ivan would be furious. They were only supposed to spy on her. Dimitri had been Ivan's favorite. Business would suffer. There wasn't supposed to be any killing. This was Dmitri's fuck-up. He cringed to think of making the call. Ivan always said, "Life is hard and then you die."

A MONTH LATER, in the weak afternoon light, two men looked out across the acres of scrub pasture and stunted trees marked at irregular intervals with metal stakes, numbers and letters painted vertically on them in some arcane system. The older man in a gray work uniform peered at a clipboard and clucked his tongue.

"I hope he's not in that washout. We still haven't sorted that mess out. Coffins and bodies were, um, disturbed. It's a work in progress I'm afraid."

Ivan, dressed in a dark, expensive overcoat and a leather hat with furred earflaps, held a slip of paper with a number on it. "I want him found."

~O~

S1:E13

The party was spread out over the top floor of the brownstone. Every light bulb had been replaced with either blinking Christmas tree lights or black lights. Bottles of champagne and cases of beer were stacked inside the front door. Someone had brought a gallon of what was supposed to be authentic moonshine. It could have been dry cleaning fluid for all anyone knew, but the hostess had poured half of the gallon into a punch bowl with a bottle of prune juice and floated chunks of frozen pineapple in it as if daring people to drink it.

There were pot brownies, a small bowl of magic mushrooms, and a platter of fresh fruit which Jack hoped was untainted. A little sign on the bowl of mushrooms read "1 per customer", a thoughtful warning he had suggested to the hostess. He made a sandwich from two large brownies and a strawberry. Health food.

Catering this bash had been done over the phone and through a messenger service and now he needed to settle up with Wendy before he could get down to any serious partying. There were twenty or so girls milling around the apartment, and he played telephone with a few of them looking for her.

A chorus of "Wendy, Jack is here," circled the room twice while he leaned against a wall smiling patiently. After a few minutes, a petite Asian girl walked up to him and slapped him on the chest with a fat envelope.

"She's busy, but she said you should count it and she'll look for what's left of you later."

Jack took the envelope. "Tell her I said she's saving the best for last."

Business settled, he put half the cash in a stamped envelope addressed to his post office box, went downstairs to the foyer, and dropped it in the outgoing mail. This was where he could have walked out the door and headed home. He thought about the rainbow of women upstairs and punched the UP button on the elevator.

The air in the apartment was blue with marijuana. Girls were dancing together intimately. It looked like he'd walked in on a pagan spring rite. Every square inch of counter space in the working kitchen was covered with food or drink. He looked dubiously at the punchbowl and settled for a shot of cheap tequila as a jumping-off point for everything else that evening—animal, vegetable, mineral, or chemical.

The ladies all belonged to some sorority; Greek was Greek to Jack, and they looked like they popped out of the same mold with little variation. Jack plunged in.

Unknown hours later, he came to at a low level of consciousness thinking he'd gone blind—no great shock given the chemical cliffhanging he'd been doing. After a minute or two of lying still checking his own pulse, his eyes adjusted to the blacklight, and he found he could focus as long as he didn't move his head. Then there was the deafness. He couldn't hear anything because he was flat on his back on the lush carpet, his arms pinned by a woman's legs, his head between her soft thighs. She was not dead because she was still warm.

He would have laughed, but someone was giving him a blowjob. He seriously hoped it was a woman, then remembered that he seemed to be the only male at the party and had started to feel like the guest of honor at a cannibal picnic.

Jack croaked, "Water, for the love of God. Water!" He struggled to sit up and spent a few moments watching a girl with a long brown ponytail and gold studs edging her ear work on his flagging cock. She was giving it all she had. He reached out and tapped her shoulder.

"Honey, I'm sure you could raise the dead on a bad day, but Jackson and I have had it for a while. If I don't get something to drink and take a piss in the next two minutes, I'm gonna choke on my tongue."

She sat up, pouted, and let him stagger to his feet. "Down the hall on the left."

He was sure he had been in a bathroom at some point in the evening. Or had he pissed in a closet somewhere? And where the fuck were his clothes?

The door to this bathroom was ajar, the light on, but Jack wasn't shy and didn't care. Water was running behind the glass door, and he wasted no time getting in and standing under the warm torrent with his mouth open wide. A shower was a good place to puke if need be, but he was feeling pretty good, revived almost, and looked around for soap.

The toilet flushed, and he instinctively stepped out of the spray to avoid getting scalded and wiped the steam off the inside of the glass door in time to watch a tall, slender woman with short, fiery red hair and breasts like apples, pull her t-shirt off and reach for the shower door. He'd not seen this one so far. This had to be Wendy.

"You must be Jack." She looked him up and down. "We're so glad you stayed."

Jack leaned against the tiles, smiled, and said, "How glad?"

Without another word, she sank to her knees and took up where the other girl had left off. The shower had done him a little good, but not enough to impress her. Still, he had hope.

"That's it honey, easy, easy. Pazienza." More to himself than her, he added, "You could give Ponytail out there lessons." She yanked her mouth away from him with more than a touch of teeth and stood up.

"Ouch, girl." Jack flinched. "What the fuck?"

"Who did you say?" Her voice boomed in the tile stall making his head throb.

"Long brunette ponytail, row of gold beads in one ear." Jack made the crazy gesture with his finger to the side of his head. Big Red slapped his face hard. She stared down on him from what seemed like a towering height. *Jeez. She didn't look so tall on her knees.* He fell back against the wall and slid down the tile holding his face as she bolted. He'd gotten the news the moment her hand contacted his face. Ponytail was supposed to be *her* girlfriend.

Wendy was cursing like a sailor as she wrenched her clothing over wet skin. She opened the shower door wide and cut off the hot water.

"Yeah, yeah. I get the picture," Jack said, as he scrambled out of the freezing spray.

. . .

THE WINDOWS of the brownstone were vibrating with the volume of the music inside. Gord was surprised that the police hadn't been by yet, but then again, it was Friday night. He leaned against the trunk of the limo and smoked his last cigarette. The shiny, black Lincoln was double-parked, completely blocking the narrow side street. He was ten minutes early for the pickup and he knew the wait could run an hour. As soon as he finished the butt, he'd think about circling the block again.

A guy came out the front door and paused at the top of the stairs to survey the street then take a hit from a fat joint. Gord laughed to himself. 'So, it's that kind of party.' It wasn't the weed he was laughing about.

It was late April and still on the brisk side at almost midnight, but the dude was buck naked except for one sock puddled around his ankle, and what Gord hoped was a wildly fringed purple, green and gold French tickler on his cock and not a serious social disease. Naked Guy seemed unconcerned or maybe unaware that he was standing naked on a lower west side stoop.

A window opened on the third floor and a work boot sailed down, landing on the sidewalk with a solid thud. Naked Guy came to a semblance of attention and looked up just as the second boot and a bundle of clothing dropped onto the stairs.

"Thanks," he called up to the open window. "Deeply appreciated and all that." The bundle rolled down the stairs and came apart, shedding a denim jacket, a t-shirt, jeans, and the other sock.

Gord asked, "Is the party starting to break up?"

Naked Guy had followed the rolling ball of clothes down to the sidewalk. "I don't think so. The acid was a little slow to lift off."

Gord groaned. "Great." His fantasy of falling into his bed before three in the morning vanished.

No shorts had rained down from above. The dude picked up the jeans, pulled them on, and suddenly noticed his gaudily clad dick hanging out of the open zipper like a refugee from a mummer's parade. "Jesus Christ! Is that mine?" he said, looking down at his crotch, wonderment and horror in his voice.

"Unless they were giving 'em out as party favors, I guess it's the one you came with," observed Gord, but no-longer Naked Guy had already gone on to the next item of acute interest - the whereabouts of his wallet.

After patting himself down twice and coming up empty, the partygoer gazed off into space like he was reading a checklist on the dashboard of a rocket ship until he suddenly pounced on one of the boots. Smiling broadly, he pulled a bloated, leather wallet from the depths of the boot and tried to tuck it in the front pocket of his jeans only to be startled a second time by his latex-embellished penis still taking the night air.

"Sonofabitch!" He grabbed the end of the fanciful rubber and pulled hard, stretching it about a foot before it snapped free and flew, landing on the roof of the limo. "Ow. Shit. Fuck!" he yelled, doubling over in pain. After a minute he stood up, zipped himself in carefully, and asked, "Dude, can I get a ride?"

Gord had pulled a broken curtain rod from a trash can and was trying to fish the rubber off the roof of the car without touching the paint. "I already got a fare," he said, over his shoulder, "One of these days."

"I'll give you double whatever they were paying. Cash."

"Did they leave you any?"

Jack went blank again for a moment, then snatched the

other boot off the sidewalk and pulled a roll of bills the size of a fist from down in the toe. The outer bill was a C-note, as was the next.

"You won't throw up in the car, right?" Gord said.

"Not if you let me ride up front."

"Are you holding?"

"Not anymore." Jack grinned and waggled the money.

There was the sound of breaking glass and they looked up in time to see a chrome toaster arc out over the car and smash a storefront window on the opposite side of the street. An alarm went off somewhere inside that building and they imagined distant sirens.

"Who were you waiting for?" Jack was staggering in circles trying to pull on the second boot.

"I don't know. Some sorority girls."

"Huh. How many?"

"Five, six. Whoever would fit back there." Gord put his fists on his hips. "You want me to wait for them too?"

"Hmm." There was a long pause while No Longer Naked-Guy considered the idea, one hand searching through his long, wet hair like he was looking for ticks. Finally, he said, "Nah. I probably had half of them already and the other half's pissed about it. It was pretty wild and degenerate up there. These chicks know how to party."

Gord succeeded in hooking the gaudy rubber with the curtain rod. "Good thing you had protection," he said as he flicked it into the street. Another crash came as a champagne bottle hit the sidewalk and exploded. Gord jumped in the car and started it. "That's it. Time to fly. I can't afford a new paint job. Get in, Cash. Where are we headed?"

"Home." Jack got in the front seat, peeled two hundred-dollar bills off the roll, and passed them to Gord who looked at them, eyebrows raised.

"Where's home, Cape Cod?" Gord said as he stashed the money in his jacket.

"How would I know where you live?" mumbled Jack. He was drifting off.

Gord sighed and put the car in gear reminding himself that one cash-paying, relatively quiet customer was better than five or six drunken, credit card waving, pissed off women any night. As the car surged forward, Jack opened his eyes, "Hey, my man. Do me a favor?"

"Depends." In the rearview mirror, blue lights lit up an intersection at the far end of the street.

Jack said, "On second thought..."

Gord hit the gas and the limo lurched down the block. He blew through the stop sign and hung a left.

Jack opened the window, leaned his face into the night air and continued with that second thought. "Hey, do you know where St. Vincent's is?"

"Yeah, not far. It's just off Jackson Square. You're not sick, are you?" Gord didn't want to have to clean puke out of the front seat, much less the back.

His passenger seemed to come back into focus and said, "Pleased to meet you."

"What?"

"Jackson. Name's Jackson. I ain't sick but I gotta go see somebody at the hospital."

"Gordon Becker." They shook hands awkwardly as Gord made the turn onto the hospital block. "Do you want me to wait? I mean you paid for the night and then some."

"Park it and come in with me. I may need some help with this."

"As long as it ain't a heist or a buy," Gord muttered, thinking about his probation.

Jack leaned over a water fountain inside the entrance,

drank deeply, splashed water in his face, and pulled his hair back, twisting it into a knot. He looked reasonably sober when he stopped a nurse and asked for directions to the Nursery.

Gord said, "Shit man, congratulations!"

"Yeah, thanks, but hold the thought. I can't even remember what she looked like other than she's another damn redhead, but she had my old address. There's going to be blood tests or some shit." He fumbled a crumpled sheet of paper out of his pocket. "If it wasn't for this official invite from welfare, I wouldn't even have her last name."

Both men pressed their foreheads to the glass. There were only a few babies visible through the viewing window. A nurse with a clipboard came out closing the door behind her soundlessly. She cast a grim eye over them. Jack tried on a smile he thought would charm. "Excuse me, ma'am. Could you point out Mary Delaney's baby?"

"Are you family?" she said, scowling. "It's after visiting hours."

"Old friend." Jack shoved the letter deeper into his pocket.

"Good of you to stop by," she sniffed without a trace of sarcasm. "Mary Delaney, redhead, about five foot two?"

Jack nodded. "Yeah, that sounds like her, I guess. It's been a while since my last shore leave."

The nurse looked Jack up and down and snorted. "Nine months, give or take? Wait right here."

She went back inside the nursery and wheeled a bassinet to the window. All they could see was a blue blanket. Gord punched Jack on the shoulder. "You got a boy!" Jack winced and jammed his fists into his pockets.

The nurse pushed the basket closer to the window and gently turned down the blanket. The baby, lips locked on a pacifier, wrinkled his brow, and wriggled slowly like a grub at the disturbance. The nurse poked her head out of the door and hissed, "The father was here this afternoon. I believe they're getting married this weekend." The door whispered shut and she wheeled the bassinet away from the window without a look back. Jack was already headed down the hall.

Stumbling to catch up, Gord said, "What would you have done if he turned out to be yours?"

Jack shrugged and picked up his pace. "Throw a wad of cash and run, I guess. Do I look like dad material to you?"

He'd been asking himself the same question every day since the letter turned up. Birth control was up to the girls as far as he was concerned. He'd sowed enough seed to raise a small army in the past few years and this was the only near-miss he'd heard about. Maybe he was shooting blanks. Maybe that wasn't a bad thing.

Gord said, "You should celebrate, but I think you've had enough party for one night. Where to?"

"West 110th. Looks out over the Park."

"Deal. I'll drop you off and swing back downtown for the ladies."

Jack said, "Don't mention me if you love living."

"Thanks for the warning. Never heard of you."

~O~

There was no denying who had killed the intruder; her fingerprints and those of the still-unidentified dead man were interlaced on the handle of the weapon. The blood all over Anna would prove to be from the male deceased. She said she couldn't remember what had happened and the medical examiner couldn't explain how she'd been able to decapitate a grown man. Luck? The short sword was not the optimal weapon for the task, in his opinion.

Within ten minutes of Anna's call for help—it was a nice neighborhood until people started subletting to clutches of college students—uniformed police swarmed first the building, then the block. The street was jammed with marked cars which were moved to make room for forensics and the coroner's vehicles. Beat cops closed the streets and TV news trucks circled the block like vultures.

The first officer on the ground-floor scene—a ten-year veteran—had slipped in Karen's blood, stumbled over her body, then vomited in the corner of the lobby in front of the mailboxes. When the responding officers kicked in the apartment door and crept into the tiny kitchen, guns drawn, Anna didn't respond for some moments, the phone still in her hand, her left arm limp by her side. She couldn't lift her arm and cried out in pain once the EMTs helped her stand up. Later, doctors would diagnose torn muscles and ligaments, and a slight shoulder separation.

There was a man's body on the floor of the adjacent bedroom. His head was on the pillow beside a female victim on the bed, blood from both the dead pooled and splashed everywhere.

Anna was only at the police station an hour before a judge remanded her to a private psychiatric facility for the duration of the investigation, the stay to be overseen by her family doctor. Doc Cohen drove up to Greenhaven with Murph and Tam and they took turns staying with Anna around the clock as she slept under a cloud of medication, her arm immobilized in a sling. A staff doctor told them that her injury was probably a result of the extreme exertion it had taken to defend herself. He'd seen the coroner's photos of the dead man and still had trouble reconciling that much violence with the girl in his care.

Murph went to each of the funerals, met with the families and the police. Tam boxed up Anna's few belongings she found in the apartment. After a week, Anna sent them home. Ray never called or came by the hospital even though he made a point of driving up to meet with the police, making sure he wasn't implicated in any way.

Killing the man had been unavoidable. Anna knew she should feel guilty about the girls, but she'd always rejected guilt as a waste of energy unless she was directly responsible for something. Had the killer been the one leaving the notes? No one alive knew about them; she never told the police. What could they have done? That Maryann had dated the man briefly also seemed moot. The fact that Ray might have known the man nagged at her, but not enough to get in touch with him. He hadn't visited or called, and Anna was fine with it. Let the dead lie quietly. In the stretch of events, it was not her fault that Karen, Netty, and Maryann were dead at the hands of a maniac, and she'd survived. There was nothing she could have done to change the outcome except become a victim herself.

GREENHAVEN WAS A MINIMUM-SECURITY FACILITY, more like a fenced hotel than a mental hospital. Inmates wore their own clothing and took their meals in a sunny dining room with waiters who wore scrubs and badges on lanyards. Still, every door in the place was locked and overseen by a changing guard of orderlies who observed the patients while discretely taking notes on their clipboards.

Anna leaned against the wall in the hallway waiting her turn at the payphone. Time for her to make the weekly call that she promised Murph. He'd be having breakfast at the bar at this time of day and Billy accepted the charges before the operator could finish asking. "How ya doing, hon? Lemme get him." He dropped the handset on the bar and Murph repeated the question when he picked it up moments later.

She used her stock, well-rehearsed answer. "New week, same stuff. Nuts everywhere, but at least they're well-medicated nuts."

"No, kiddo. How are you doing?" She knew Murph wouldn't settle for the news and the weather today, and she struggled to keep the conversation light.

"I sleep because of the pills. I can't eat because of the pills. I miss everyone." Tears were close, but she'd be damned if she would upset him by crying and she slipped back into sarcasm. "Sarah Nightingale's evil twin works here, but she's cool. Wants me to do a reading for her."

"Watch yourself, kiddo," he said. "Don't be giving them anything they can use. Now, listen, you're gonna meet someone today or tomorrow. A lawyer."

She cut him off. "Murph, I thought we agreed that getting a lawyer would look bad? I can do this time, it's only months." Murph had his doubts.

"This is something different. Not any kind of plea or anything. He knows what he's doing. Name's Rockwell. He'll introduce himself and tell you what you need to know."

Anna sighed. More than anything else she wanted to get off the institutional regimen of medication. The rotation of pills with each meal left her feeling like her head was stuffed with dirty wool socks. She could do a better job of managing her own drugs. The sooner she could leave, the better. "Okay, Murph. We'll do it your way. Give Tam a hug for me. Yeah. I know. I will." As she hung up, someone behind her cleared his throat loudly and said, "Any day, sweetheart."

She frowned down on the moon-faced man next in line. He had an orderly's smock on over hospital pajamas and penny loafers instead of slippers. He was balding, short, and stocky and she'd seen him muttering into the payphone, a sheaf of papers in his hand and a couple ballpoint pens leaking into his shirt pocket.

He took off his horn-rimmed glasses and said, "Anna Catalano, right? Save me a seat at lunch."

IN THE FIRST week after the murders, Murph met several times with the lead detective, a Lt. Daniel Delgado. "A whiff of the climber to him, a DA wannabe," Murph concluded. "You need to be careful around him, Anna. The newspapers were in a froth about the murders for a couple days, but since the killer's dead, so's the story, but this Delgado is looking to make a name for himself."

The identity of the dead man—it was still undetermined if he alone was responsible for killing all three of the girls—remained a mystery. There was no match for his prints in the system locally or with the FBI. No one came forward to claim the body and he would be buried in an unmarked grave by the end of the month.

Detective Delgado visited Anna every Sunday after she was admitted, bringing her magazines and the Sunday *New York Times*. He had her sketchbook and was impressed with her skill as he went around interviewing her classmates and teachers; her drawings were exacting likenesses. The most recent sketch bothered him, though. No one he spoke with seemed to know the face and yet, it was somehow familiar. He was sitting at his desk, leafing through the sketchbook, and reading his notes when it came to him; the strikingly handsome face—strong jaw, long dark hair, piercing eyes, full lips—looked a little like the killer. Could he possibly get so lucky? He took the sketchbook to the morgue.

The attendant looked at Anna's sketch, then down at Dmitri's bloodless face, his head held in place on the stainless-steel tray by a strap of bandage taped across his forehead. They had not bothered stitching the head back onto the body.

"Another fucking rock star carved like a Christmas ham." He cocked his head and looked from the corpse to the drawing and back again. "Close, but no cigar, if she's as good as you say. This one is younger, heavier," he tapped the drawing with a gloved finger. "Maybe he's just her type, eh?" He elbowed Delgado in the ribs.

In the weeks following the murders, Daniel took some heat about the amount of time he was spending at Greenhaven. His partner was running out of patience with him. "Tsk. Tsk, Danny boy. Romancing a suspect is a terrible idea. You should know better."

Daniel told himself that he did know better, but Anna pulled on him in ways he didn't understand, and even though it troubled him, he kept going back. She was beautiful, aloof, unapproachable, but most of all, a suspect. Given the circumstances, he knew the death of the unknown man would be ruled an act of self-defense, although some might call it murder. So much boiled down to 'why' and Anna seemed to have no useful answers and he'd mostly stopped asking.

When they were together, talking about nothing at all, she warmed to him, and he felt what he imagined heroin would be like. When she laughed, he would lose his train of thought and she teased him and called him a space cadet. His *Abuela* would say he was bewitched.

In the beginning, Daniel would ask her oblique questions about the crime, but she had nothing for him. The doctors put her memory loss down to the trauma. Other times, like today, they would just talk; bemoaning their respective hometown baseball teams, talking books, movies, the weather, never coming near what he really wanted to talk about. It was a dance with an acre of lush pasture between the dancers. A no-man's-land of possibilities he didn't dare cross. The longing was there, but never the will.

Daniel returned the sketchbook to Anna and watched without comment as she leafed through the pages. When she got to the last one, he said, "I didn't find this guy on campus or in the neighborhood. Do you know him?"

Anna reflected on the encounter. "I was working on a paper at the library. At first, I thought he was a homeless guy, maybe." She looked at the wall, calling up the details from her memory. "He sat at the opposite end of the table from me. I wasn't bothered, all the tables were occupied, two, three people. He was purposeful, asked me for a piece of paper. Copied some stuff out of the newspaper and left." She didn't mention the vodka. The aching homesickness that compelled her to flirt with the stranger welled up and tried to reclaim her like a tide coming in. Her eyes filled with tears, but the medications braked her feelings. All her feelings.

Delgado was charming and good-looking; a genuine tall, dark, and handsome. Even from behind her medicated veil, Anna could sense his interest in her went beyond the case. It was a relief to deal with him on a normal basis, not knowing what he was thinking about her. It would have been so easy to let their rapport—they had been on a first-name basis from the start—drift into something like romance. She was equal parts terrified and drawn to him.

On one hand, she was flattered by his attention. On the other, she was afraid that he was just working her as a suspect. Murph said the cops would do that, act the friend, and trick you into spilling something they could use against you. She considered her uncle's long career at the edges of the law and the fact that he had never seen the inside of a jail cell. The last thing she needed was the law in her life any more than it already was.

At the end of her third month in the hospital, Daniel arranged to meet her in one of the small gardens on the hospital grounds. He never asked what she wanted but always brought tea in cardboard takeout cups and a bag of churros. This time, she made a point of wearing a dress, fussing her hair into line and putting on a little makeup. He usually just showed up without warning. Of course, he had to know she was being released before she found out. *Damned drugs!* She played her part anyway.

"Daniel! They are letting me go home."

He smiled and handed her a cup. "Yeah, I heard. That's why I'm here. Well, partly. And to say goodbye."

Even though she was certain there was no romance in their future, she hadn't anticipated goodbye. She wanted something else from the moment, but what?

"I've been doing this a while now," Daniel said. "Seen a lot of bad things done by a lot of bad people. You consider everything and everyone at the scene and you think you know what went down. Then, something like this comes along," he tapped the case file on his lap, "and I question what I've been doing and why." He sipped his tea and shook his head. "The worst ones never get caught. Not by us anyway."

Anna was chewing the dry pastry and suddenly had a hard time swallowing the gritty sugar.

Daniel continued, "So I'm here to let you know that the investigation is officially closed. You won't be held responsible or charged with the man's death in any way and you're free to leave the jurisdiction, if and when you choose to do so."

The last part he read off formally like the Miranda warning he'd read her in the interrogation room after the murders. Even then he'd been kind to her. He stood and extended his hand. She hesitated but held out her hand, sticky with sugar. She didn't trust herself to speak, but her smile betrayed her.

"I wish you well, Anna," he said. "I wish...". The handshake held.

All she wanted was for him to take her in his arms, but he didn't, and she stood her lonely ground, aching with embarrassment for him and said, "I know."

He covered their clasped hands with his other and looked into her eyes. "Take care of yourself out there in the world. Watch yourself." He had given up and she was just a little sad about it.

Anna watched Daniel walk away and as soon as he disappeared through the gate, she wiped her eyes on her sleeve and said, "Anything else you want to know Rock?" Rocky had been eavesdropping from a bench nearby.

The short, balding man scuttled up to sit beside her on the bench.

"Shh!" he said, looking around. "You can't be too careful!" Then he crossed his legs at the knee and wrapped his arms around his chubby belly and rocked back and forth, his subtlest crazy routine.

"You don't have to lay it on thick for me." She knew there wasn't a thing wrong with him. He was a character actor at heart and looked at this stint inside as a paid vacation. There were potential clients everywhere. Rocky did things his way.

Once it was clear that Anna would not be facing criminal proceedings, he handled the case with the gusto of a vulture, suing everyone in sight from the college to the Neighborhood Watch on her behalf. Anna was unconvinced but went along. To her surprise, it was the brownstone owners who caved. The security intercom had been broken for months.

Rocky said, "Here. Got a present for you. No, don't open it here, wait until you are on the sidewalk. They could still confiscate it." He passed her a bulky envelope. "Stow it and don't open it until I tell you to."

By that afternoon, her release interview was over, and she was packed, composed, and ready to leave. Her case manager told her that a cab would be waiting at the gate at 3:30 sharp. From there, she was on her own. Anna decided to wait to tell Tam and Murph. Surprise them even. There had been a small farewell party in the garden at lunch, complete with cake and ice cream. Rocky sat next to her, consuming a huge piece of sheet cake and spooning ice cream off her plate. He nudged her and whispered,

"There'll be papers coming to your address in Connecticut. You'll need a witness and a notary, then throw it all back in the mail and it's done. Five G's is not a lot of money, but it'll get you started once you make a break for it."

"I don't know how to thank you."

"You don't have to." He looked around the room furtively, licked his plate and said, "I got my third and a half dozen new clients." He jiggled all over with barely suppressed giggling.

An orderly called from the doorway to the garden. "Anna, your ride is here. Rocky where's my five dollars?"

Rocky was convulsed with laughter. "Her ride, he says," as they followed the man in white scrubs out to the street.

Anna gave Rocky an awkward hug. "You better start taking those meds." Outside the gate, she looked up and down the block but there was no sign of a cab. Behind her, on his side of the chain-link fence, Rocky advised, "Open it now, dummy. The envelope!"

Inside the envelope, she found a hundred dollars in cash, a cashier's check for five thousand dollars, and a set of car keys. She scrutinized the check. It looked real enough. It looked like Rocky was the real deal after all. She'd had her doubts. She held up the keys and looked at him, puzzled.

"Over there. The black one." He was gleeful. "I'm so fucking jealous." Across the street, a 1970 Chevelle SS, black with wide, white stripes on the hood and glittering chrome wheels, sat like a dragon holding its breath.

Without a look back, she unlocked the door, tossed her bag in the back and then, as if they were old friends, keyed the dragon to life. She revved the engine and turned out of the parking spot facing the car the wrong way on a one-way street so she could pull up to the curb in front of Rocky. He was jumping up and down behind the fence clapping his hands. She tried to imagine him wearing a suit in court but couldn't. She revved the engine harder, rolled down her window and yelled, "Let me know when you are getting out and I'll spring you."

He yelled back. "Hell no! I'm gonna have a red one!"

She gunned it to the end of the block, turned and was gone.

Anna made her way back to New York and, out of sad habit, back to Ray. He was careful with her in the beginning. Solicitous almost. He gave her the space he thought she needed, even his half of the double bed most nights. He slept in a used leather recliner in the living room. A miserable detente. He made sure she had everything she needed by way of drugs or alcohol.

TIME PASSED WITH LITTLE CHANGE. She got a job working part-time at the county courthouse and found some regular Tarot clients. Occasionally, she spent Sundays at the farm with Tam and Murph. There was no talk of returning to college. Some nights she'd take the Chevelle out of the garage and put miles on it going nowhere in particular. The next day she would spend time washing the car and ignoring Ray as he harangued her about the cost of gas and the risks of driving impaired.

At first, she was content to let life happen a day at a time. She watched TV next door with their neighbors and friends, got high, took pills, drank, and fell asleep on one couch or another.

She put up with Ray's occasional demands for her to attend dinners or business meetings. In the beginning, he only half-believed her observations. Life was small, safe, boring, and lonely. The days stretched out ahead of her like a blank slate until Ray started making his problems hers, and life turned cold and dark.

~O~

Despite the rawness of the spring morning, she opened all the windows, letting the cold air sweep through the apartment. Barefoot, she stood swaddled in a ragged quilt in front of the stove watching the coffee trickle down inside the glass percolator. The cold didn't matter. It was the fresh air she needed. The nightly sleeping pills were lingering until lunch, and she knew she'd have to quit cold turkey soon. There would be no tapering off.

She filled a mug and breathed in the steam. Doctored it with half and half and honey, then swilled half the cup as hot as she could stand it. She suspected this was how alcoholics felt about their first drink of the day. The curtains moved with the breeze, and she could see a bee, sluggish with the chill, making his way down through the folds.

From a basket on the table, she took a worn Tarot deck, snapped off the rubber band and drew one card, putting it face down on the table by her cup. Another sip and she flipped the card over. The Hanged Man.

"Hmmff. Tell me something I don't already know," her tone more wistful than sarcastic. This card and others with a similar message had been showing up all too often for her to ignore them. "Wait," the cards advised. "Give up trying to control everything." The bee had crawled from the curtains to the table and was making his way across the expanse of wood to the cards. *What everything? My life? Wait for what?*

"Thanks for nothing today," she said, as she tucked the card back into the deck and finished the coffee. Other people paid for her advice through the cards, but she rarely followed any for herself.

The bee ignored both the cards and the dot of honey that had dripped onto the table. Bees didn't bother Anna, so she watched as it disappeared under her left wrist, tasting her skin with its antenna. It climbed onto the back of her hand and rested there absorbing her warmth. She put her head down on the table to get a closer look wondering if it was a worker from the hive in the wall or a wild stranger in the neighborhood.

Ray yelled from the hollow of the hallway behind her, "I don't know what time I'll be back." He slammed the door.

Startled, the bee arched its abdomen and plunged its stinger into the shadow of a vein on the back of her hand. She saw it coming and held still, assessing the level and nature of the pain as the venom sped through her bloodstream. Rather than leap away from her which would kill it as the barb and its internal organs stayed planted in her skin, the bee hunkered down, clutching at fine hairs, savoring her warmth.

Her eyes watered and tears spilled. The pain was a distant thrill and the flavors and smells of the coffee and honey in her mouth and nose intensified. At that moment, she and the bee were good for each other. The bee was doomed, but as far as she could tell, he wasn't worried about it.

．　．　．

EVERYONE LIES *and lies about lying.* It was her job to get to the bottom of people. Where they were and how they got there. People could shape their own futures to a degree, but there wasn't a damn thing they could do about their past, least of all hide it from Annabea Catalano.

It was the first day of *voir dire*—the cattle call where all the players gathered for her inspection to be branded and culled, depending on which side was paying her. She didn't work for the defense if she knew the defendant had committed violent, high-profile crimes, no matter what the money. Dirty money carried its freight of bad karma. There was the press to consider, too. The last thing she needed was the possibility of seeing herself on TV or in print associated with some blatantly guilty asshole who got acquitted on one of her cases.

This defendant had been arrested and charged with a string of non-violent felonies from selling fake IDs and receiving stolen property, to his latest venture, grand theft auto. A fucking hearse, of all things, complete with an expensive casket. He was a three-time loser and headed for a long, perhaps interminable stretch of time in federal prison unless his lawyer could snake him out of the whole thing and Attorney Thomas Olaghieri was a master of snaking. Anna made a point of never meeting the defendant and avoiding eye contact once they were in the courtroom. On paper, they were just criminals who got caught. When no one was looking they might be fiends of a more heinous stripe and she didn't want to know.

She knew what was at stake in this case and charged accordingly; a thousand dollars for what might take two or three days at most. Cash. No guarantees and certainly no explanations, but she had no doubt that Olaghieri had investigated her track record, as best he could. She was mostly a rumor. Her repeat clients hoarded her.

To the casual observer, she was a sketch artist, working from behind whatever legal team was paying for her time. She always started the first day with a flattering view of the judge just in case he or she called Anna on her presence in the room, but it had never come to that.

As each juror was called, she held the pad so all they could see was her eyes. The strategy to force their eyes never failed—they always looked right at the artist sketching them. She'd make steady eye contact for a long moment and then lick her lips and look away. The subject, male or female, it didn't matter, would do the same. It wasn't necessary for her to get a read, but it helped her focus if they met her halfway. One by one, she was careful with them, unobtrusive.

No matter how they cuddled the Bible and swore to tell the truth, Anna knew what each one was really thinking and feeling about the defendant, the case, and the lawyers. People had their reasons and Anna found them out. Unfortunately, useful information came with back-stories.

People loved to wallow in their personal misery. They replayed the litany of their failures, defeats, and sorrows like theme music. Each time she read someone she got whatever was preoccupying their thoughts, the emotional colors the subject was experiencing, and there was something about jury duty that brought out the worst in people. Fear, anger, and anxiety were big on the hit parade and Anna felt all of them when she was working someone. It was exhausting, but short of hooking or robbing banks, the money was worth it. So far. She wished the art paid as well. Working strictly in graphite on white paper, her style was stark, the likenesses almost photographic. She never parted with a single drawing and, once the trial was over, she burned them.

For court, she had a frumpy-to-invisible guise down pat. With her hair pulled back into a low-slung lump on the back of her neck, she wore a dark turtleneck under an ill-fitting jacket paired with a straight skirt that fell two inches below her knees. Dark stockings, Maryjane's, and no makeup or jewelry. Her friend and neighbor, Gabriel, joked that she looked like an Italian grandmother in training. It worked. No one ever looked at her twice or remembered seeing her.

While they waited for the judge to show up, Olaghieri didn't recognize her. She was sitting right behind him and snickered as he scanned the room looking for her. He was looking right over her head when she stuck out her tongue at him. He made puzzled eye contact, Anna nodded and said very softly, "That's right, it's me, asshole. Turn around and sit down." His eyes bugged, but he did as she said. "Just go about your business and we'll work it just like we practiced." The judge could not see her poke him in the shoulder with a sharp fingernail when she deemed a juror unfit. She'd been adamant. No questions. Ignore her rulings and his client would suffer the consequences.

Their first meeting had been a week earlier over lunch at a small restaurant Anna picked in Manhattan. She didn't want to risk either of them being seen by someone who knew them. Low profile was the way she wanted and kept it; her services would be just another line item in a lawyer's bill.

"Wait a minute," he said, "you're saying we can't confer? I have to take what you say for granted without knowing why? How..." She put up her hand silencing him. She had that kind of power over men once they stopped gawking at her tits.

"You wouldn't have agreed to this meeting if you didn't know what to expect, so if you're not happy at this juncture," she slid the envelope with the cash back across the table to him, "we can call it good and just enjoy lunch." She fell on her steak like a construction worker.

Thomas studied her for a moment and said wryly. "I thought you were going to be easy."

Anna let the double entendre blow by. She speared a chunk of bloody steak with her fork, pointed it at him, and said, "It doesn't get any easier for you than keeping your mouth shut, does it?" She dragged the meat through a puddle of A-1 and popped it in her mouth. "Eat up. It's going to get cold." She was half hoping he would bail now. He was an arrogant tool. At their first meeting, he acted like he was sure that her fee would include a chance to fuck her. *Surprise, surprise. Take a number, idiot.*

In a world of Twiggy wannabes, she was out of step and out of style. Physically abundant, luxurious. Hair, lips, tits, legs, and ass—she got extra helpings of everything. She could have been a Playboy bunny if she had been six-foot-two, but at five-nine, men saw her as voluptuous if they were kind, and fat if they weren't. It had been a long time since a man's opinion meant anything to her. They couldn't help themselves. Like chimps.

She wasn't above appreciating a good-looking, well-dressed man, but all too often they came with a head full of ego and bad attitude. Maybe it was the company she kept, but it had been a long time since a man looked at her as anything more than a disposable piece of ass. Being trapped in a shitty marriage also took the fun out of pretending to be single.

Olaghieri had the additional, and increasingly irritating, problem of a growing cocaine habit. The vibe she got from coke users was like a TV station that had gone off the air for the night, no Star-Spangled Banner. They were impossible to read but predictable as their cravings. By now he was thinking more about the next opportunity he'd have to powder his nose than he was about her tits.

She didn't tell him that she couldn't be accurate if a subject was drunk or high on anything. It used to be a safe bet that anyone reporting for jury duty would come to court sober, but these days, anything was possible. She would disqualify anyone under the influence to protect her batting average. The shit was making her job difficult. They continued eating in silence, Anna finishing before he did. She picked up her glass of wine, looked through it to the windows behind him and said, "Well, what's it going to be? My way or bye-bye."

Sullen, he pushed the envelope of cash across the table, and she slipped it into her purse.

"You won't be disappointed, but one more thing," she drained the glass, got up and whispered in his ear. "You can't afford my other services and do not, under any circumstance, show up in court high. I'll know and I'll walk."

He brought his napkin to his nose reflexively on the off chance that a trace of powder lingered around his nostrils and leaned out of the booth to watch her walk all the way to the front door.

~O~

S1:E16

Charlie Mack's trial was over before it started. His lawyer was late, and the judge merely called for a ten-minute recess. The judge didn't appear to be surprised or upset at the delay. Anna suspected the judge was on the take, but she didn't want to get close enough to be sure. Too much exposure.

She was looking down at the parking structure and wishing the windows could open. A late-model sedan pulled up in a big hurry, misjudged the sharp turn into the garage, and nailed a parked state police cruiser. Hard. Broken glass and shattered plastic sprayed over the cruiser and the rooftop light bar broke free and crashed to the pavement.

The sound of the impact drew half the courtroom to the windows. A man jumped out of the sedan like a chicken on a hotplate; it was Olaghieri, about to have a very bad day. Anna knew him by the precise round bald spot that he thought no one could see because he was tall. Two troopers clambered out of their almost new unit and swiftly had him in handcuffs.

The bailiff was bellowing for everyone to take their seats. After a few minutes of general disorder, a sheriff's deputy handed the judge a note and he started pounding his gavel for real, calling the court to order.

"Alright, nobody was hurt but you, Mr. Mack," the judge said, pointing his gavel at the defendant. The defendant's smirking at the interruption faded to a scowl. "You'll be remanded back to the hospitality of the state until you can find yourself another lawyer. Seems as if your current one might be sharing a cell with you since he's been arrested on a number of charges."

Anna almost laughed out loud. Easiest grand she'd ever raked down. A day with no agenda was just what she needed. With Mack and Olaghieri behind bars, she felt a sudden openness in her head that made her giddy. It wasn't that what she did to make money was so bad, in fact, it was always interesting. The legal process fascinated her. She could have been a great prosecutor if she had finished school, but that would never happen.

It was the people in the courthouse who bothered her, every single one of them wrangling for position. Everyone, except the defendant, was supposed to be honoring the legal process, the institution. But that was rarely the case. People had their own agenda and, guilty or innocent, the players never stopped gaming the system.

There was no one for her to account to for the next ten or twelve hours. No one keeping tabs or passing judgment on what she was doing, thinking, or saying. She wouldn't be speaking with anyone if she could help it. Anna could see her salvation out on the farthest corner of the top parking deck sparkling in the sunshine. She heard the smack of the gavel again and a voice yelled over the crowd noise, "Court dismissed!" She snatched up her drawing pad and slunk out of the courtroom with the crowd, breaking into a sprint as soon as she cleared the revolving doors.

She dashed up the three flights of concrete stairs to her car. The morning had been overcast and threatened rain, but now the clouds stampeded before a breeze strong enough to swirl her long skirt around her legs and dry the perspiration on her face. She took the clip out of her bun and the breeze whipped her hair around her head like a cartoon electrocution as she stood in the open door of the formidable car letting the wind blow the stale, angst-ridden air of the courtroom away from her.

The car door closed with a satisfying thud and she keyed the ignition without touching the gas pedal—in her mind, a test of a car's general health and well-being. The strong spark ready, the fuel pure desire, the energy of combustion, and the translation of that power through the mechanisms, all working smoothly with one objective–power, which, in turn, equaled speed. The big-block miracle of Detroit engineering roared to life and settled quickly into a sub-aural thrum. The car spoke to her heart. *Ready.*

Some cars had personalities and joked with her. Many complained. Some lectured. This car was so completely about power that the design didn't express gender. It had no idea that it was so beautiful; the sleek black and white graphics and shape made it look like a killer whale. She thought of it as a "he". All that muscle and everything it stood for.

She navigated the city streets carefully and, once back on the parkway, fished half a joint from a fold in her bag, gripping it with her hair clip. The silver clip was one of her prized possessions, found years ago at a yard sale someplace upstate when she and Gina were on the prowl.

An elderly woman had presided over the sale from a

rocker on the porch of a ramshackle house. Beside the rocker was a small, glass-topped jewelry case protecting the small treasures from sticky-fingered shoppers. Anna examined each item before deciding there was nothing there for her.

The old woman stopped Anna with a word. "Wait." She took a small basket from under her chair. More trinkets. Anna stirred the contents with her fingers, and the old woman's eyes darkened as Anna lifted a large silver dragonfly out of the tangle of cheap bangles and chains. "It was waiting for you, I think," the old woman said.

The engraved silver wings were four inches across, the segmented body and head as big as Anna's little finger. Where delicate legs should be underneath, two rows of serrated bone claws set onto a heavy spring promised to be strong enough to corral her mane of hair. The eyes were moonstones making the insect appear blind.

"How much?"

The old woman knew she could name her price by the look of wonder on Anna's face. "Five dollars."

"Done."

When she got it home, she cleaned it with her toothbrush dipped in Windex and discovered that the tiny front legs of the insect were also on springs and made a perfect roach clip.

Now, she cracked the window, lit up, and smoked the joint to the last ash as the car carried her up the coast. Under these circumstances, getting high was little more than cleaning her mental house of the morning tension. She burned through the buzz by the time she got to the beach. Her intention was to find a spot in the sand somewhere, fix her eyes on the waves, and let her mind take her where and whenever it wanted. To step away from who and what she was, away from the tangle of her present circumstance. For a precious few hours, freedom.

The morning was panning out so differently from what she'd expected that she felt like a helium balloon with a broken string. The world receded to the hum of the car engine and the tires conversing with the various surfaces of the road that carried them up the Connecticut coast. Soon, the tires crunched over shells and gravel as she pulled into a parking lot. The smell of the Atlantic was at its peak—salt, iron, and dead sea things all pounded together on the rocks. It affected her more than the marijuana.

There would be watchers gathered to warn and protect her from any human intrusion—not likely on a gusty weekday morning. Gulls most likely, milling about quietly unless someone approached her. Perhaps a stray dog or cat. Something to have her back while she was away from her body. She didn't call these guardians or court them, they just appeared. She'd long ago given up wondering why. They were just animals. Maybe it was a smell or a vibe she had. They never bothered her, so she no longer paid much attention.

She took an old quilt from the trunk, her sketchpad, and a stick of graphite, and tucked the keys in her bra. Just above the tide line—a foot-wide band of tangled dead seagrass, wort, and human detritus—she settled the quilt on the bone-dry sand, gathered her hair into a knot, and re-fixed the silver dragonfly. Straight-backed and cross-legged, long skirt tucked under her feet and hands cupping her knees, she took three deep, slow breaths exhaling each one slower than the first. Time passed with the clouds.

A loud grunt from beside her startled her back into awareness. An hour had disappeared, the sun, higher in the sky, the clouds gone. The heat was baking her head and there was a strong smell of fish in the air. Not five feet away a large seal lay on the sand. She quelled the impulse to scream and scramble away and held very still as the creature watched her through slitted eyes. Fast moves would not be good for either of them.

Its fur was mottled gray and black, sleek, and shiny. The beast was stretched out, chin on the sand, his oily-looking eyes on her, nostrils, and whiskers busy with her change of status. He rolled over on his back slowly and closed his eyes, pretending to ignore her. Upside down, his black lips pulled back revealing rows of razor-sharp teeth. He heaved a great sigh, grunted, and rolled another quarter turn, dismissing her with his back. Quietly, she turned to a clean page in the sketch pad and began drawing her latest guardian.

With another grunt, he suddenly brought his entire front end upright, looked in her direction for a moment, then lurched for the shoreline with an impossibly fluid roll of skin, bone, and muscle. One moment he was snoring beside her, and the next, his tail flicked from the light surf as he submerged and took off on more important business. Moments later, the reason for his hasty departure came over the rise from the parking lot.

A squad of young children, all less than waist high, boiled over the crest of the beach, tumbling, squealing, dragging baskets and plastic pails down to the exact spot the seal just vacated. The sand was probably still warm.

Anna couldn't help but smile. She liked children, for the most part, the younger the better. Their little minds were occupied with the simplest things. Needs, wants, fears. Everything real and immediate. Few of them imagined beyond their age. This batch was focused on the fun of sand and surf. But children almost always came along with the freight of parents, people usually overloaded with worry, anxiety, or resentment at the staggering responsibilities of parenting and marriage, and she made a point of keeping her distance.

A moment later, they appeared. A man and woman, grim in their determination to pretend to be a happy family having a rare weekday outing at the beach. Before anyone could strike up a conversation, Anna gathered up her things and left.

~O~

S1:E17

Speed didn't go out much anymore. He couldn't tolerate the noise or the bustle of the city, but then he didn't have to. Anything he needed or wanted he paid for in cash and had brought to his apartment. Jack had never been there. They used to conduct their business by phone and in small restaurants all over the city. The last time he'd seen Speed was the week before he'd been busted and shuffled off to the Navy.

The dealer had fronted Jack pounds of premium marijuana since Jack was in eighth grade, but it wasn't Jack's skills as a salesman that the man prized. It was the resellers that Jack vetted for him. Five of his top six people had come to him through Jack. Every one of them fully solid, dedicated to the dollar. Ruthless businessmen and women. As far as Speed was concerned, if Jack vouched for you, you were gold. Now Jack was back and giving him trouble. Speed wanted to see him and find out why.

Jack waited two days after picking up his messages to call Speed back, knowing he was probably stoking the man's paranoia and anger. Speed wanted Jack to come to his penthouse fortress.

"I ain't coming up there, man. Meet me in the park," Jack said.

"What the fuck you mean? What park? Since when you such a nature boy?"

"You pick the park, I don't care. I'll give you that."

"You give me?" Speed was incredulous.

"Take it or leave it, man." Jack hung up and leaned back into the hinge of the folding glass door. The phone rang before he could light a cigarette.

They met an hour later in Washington Square which was buzzing with people taking advantage of the fine early spring weather. The usual assortment of students, businesspeople, street people wandering around, all together, all very separate.

Jack picked up on Speed's problem without even reading him, which would have been impossible, anyway. "Snowblind" was an apt description of people who were using too much cocaine. They couldn't see themselves as others saw them.

Speed looked like he hadn't slept in days. Even with a fresh haircut and shave, he looked haggard. Jack knew better than to mention it. Kid gloves, for now anyway. He steeled himself for the conversation knowing the dealer would start it up. He clapped his hands together in mock merriment.

"Jack. Jesus. I almost didn't recognize you, kid. You grew! Join the Navy and see the world, eh?"

"I worked in the base bakery in Maryland for two years," Jack replied dryly. "I can do bitchin' biscuits for four hundred. What do you want?"

"Good. Good. Right to the point. Time is money, right? Speed jittered in place.

Jack dug his fists into his jacket pockets and edged back a half step. The man's buzz was giving him a pain behind his eyes and a sour metallic taste in his mouth like he'd licked a leaky battery.

Speed closed the distance between them and put a sweaty hand on Jack's shoulder. "I need you to start taking the heavier packages, Jack. I have more customers for blow than I have sellers I can trust. All the people you brought me —Marco, Adam, Bettina—all of them are servicing very high-end clients now. I need you to step up and join them, Jack. And the money, it goes without saying. I'll make you an extremely wealthy young man in no time at all."

The money, the money, and all it could buy. But even at nineteen, Jack had the long view on wealth. Money couldn't buy him out of the singular loneliness that had been the backbeat of his life since he was a little kid. It was just a tool and putting himself in jeopardy as a coke middleman for the sake of money was nonsense and there was no way to make Speed understand.

Jack put up his hands. "Look, Speed, I told you when I got back to town that moving a little weed for you would be fun. A way to get back into the swing of things. I appreciate that you've always done me way better than wholesale, but I gotta say no to this."

Speed took out a handkerchief, wiped his eyes and blew his nose. Jack knew that he wanted to look into the handkerchief but kept himself from doing it while someone was watching. His solicitous mask of disappointment rearranged itself to one of menace tinged with desperation. "I think you've decided to go into business for yourself." He held up a hand, "Don't bother lying."

Jack searched the clouds for patience. A breeze had sprung up, and food wrappers scuttled over their feet like paper rats. He turned and walked away.

Speed shouted at his back, "I'm watching you, my friend. You've been warned."

~O~

S1:E18

Anna put herself on hold the day of the murders and still had more questions than answers about what had happened in Boston, most of all, how and why she'd survived. Without a goal or an idea of where to begin looking, she took to hiding. Going along with Ray's program was a pain in the ass, but it also served as cover.

Ray was deep into his campaign of currying favor with local union officials, petty politicians, and a variety of businessmen, all of them with sidelines of various criminal activities and all pretending to be upstanding citizens. Anna knew better. He took her along when he had meetings with potential clients, to union functions, and drug buys. He bought her clothes and made her dress up. Hair, makeup, everything to his specifications. Before setting out, she would look in the mirror and be satisfied that she did not know who that woman was.

At the end of an evening, it was always Ray asking, "What do they think about me?" She took smug delight in giving him the unvarnished truth. The people he dealt with were always looking for an in and only saw Ray as a tool, but even as she told him, he gloated. Being used was an accept-able way of getting ahead in his book.

Sifting through people's thoughts for useful information exposed Anna to their constant mental replays. People didn't drag around happy times. It was always what they had versus what they wanted, an endless litany of misery and depravity. When she read them, she experienced their fear, anger, jealousy, and all manner of sordid fantasies and imagined horrors as if she had a starring role. They became boring and predictable. It became harder and harder to shock her.

One worried about the books he'd been cooking, another about forcing his girlfriend to have another abor-tion. One man had abandoned his incapacitated mother in a nursing home somewhere in the Midwest while another dressed as a woman when he did housework. Everyone had dirty little secrets and each one was a key that Ray could use against them. He never threatened anyone with exposure. Instead, he just let them know that he knew, that he even commiserated sometimes, and made insinuations—that friends kept each other's secrets. His list of friends and donors grew. Anna was exposed to rape, sodomy, incest, bondage, torture; an ever-growing list of what the worst humanity had to offer one another.

Tonight, it was a meeting with a club owner named Garmon Portillo and the county building inspector, a doughy Irish-looking guy named Bill something. Anna didn't want to pay close attention. Just being at the table with the three of them would be hard enough. What she really wanted was a drink or a toke or two, but Ray wouldn't let her even have a cocktail until after the evening was over. After she had gotten what he came for. Sometimes he'd send her out to the car to wait for him after only a few minutes as if she was a misbehaving child.

They met at a small restaurant close to Garmon's club—the kitchen at the club was still under renovation. Garmon wanted to make some changes to the electrical system, but the county inspector wasn't on board. Ray had boasted that he could make all Garmon's low-ball shortcuts happen, and quickly. His grand opening would happen on time. Bill was waiting to see what was in it for him and busied himself eyeballing Anna's cleavage.

She sat across from Garmon at the small round table and ate like she was starving and never interrupted their conversation. Ray barely acknowledged her, and she could tell by his staring that Garmon was beginning to think she might be retarded. She burped and covered her mouth after the fact and giggled at Bill who had been trying to play footsie under the table with her all during dinner. She lunged at a passing waiter for the dessert menu.

The men jousted briefly over who would pick up the check while Anna wrapped dinner rolls in a cloth napkin and stuffed them in her purse. Once they were back in the car Ray said, "What the fuck was that all about, making a pig of yourself in there?

"I was hungry and speaking of pigs, would you like me to paint you a picture of what your friend was thinking about doing to me?"

He didn't even ask which friend she meant. "That was the whole point in dressing you up and bringing you along," he sneered. "What did you get?"

"I got tortured and bitten by dogs while he watched and jerked off. How's that?"

Ray turned his face away from her silently. She knew that if she didn't give him what he wanted in the next ten seconds, he would hit her. If she gave it up, she could count on a week of him being too busy to make any kinds of demands on her—that he might not even come home for days at a time. Still, she ran the count to nine just to watch his fury build.

"Big Bill has a wife and twin baby girls in a lovely home in White Plains. He spends a small fortune on strippers but that's about to come to an end because he has a pregnant Puerto Rican girlfriend who lives in Jersey with her mother. He met her at a club last year and now he's paying all her bills. He can't leave his wife because she owns most of his company. If the wife finds out about the girlfriend, she'll bankrupt him." Anna wrote a name and address on the back of a parking ticket. "Show him this. He'll shit his pants then play ball if you don't get greedy. Now leave me alone."

"Can I trust Portillo?" Ray pressed. *If she's right, she's worth her weight in gold, even if she puts on a few pounds eating like that. Even without sex.*

"Sure, if you want to be his butt boy. He thinks you're a stupid gringo, but he wants you to sell his drugs to your country club friends. People he has no access to. He wants you for a flunky and he'll keep giving you as much blow as you can stuff up your nose. He wants you to need him like your next line. Did you notice that he gave you his card twice? He even slipped me one behind your back," she smirked.

Ray snarled and gripped the steering wheel. Garmon had pressed a card and a gram of coke into his palm when they first shook hands and the second card as they were leaving. *Call me. Call me.* They were meeting the club's manager in a few minutes. Garmon wouldn't be there. Anna took a joint from her bag, lit it, and blew smoke in his face. "I'm off the clock as of now."

"I told you no smoking in the car!" He lowered all the power windows in the Caddy at once. Fighting with her now would not get the rest of his business with Garmon accomplished. He gritted his teeth and swore under his breath. Anna tossed the dinner rolls out the window for the rats that watched from the edges of the parking lot, eyes glittering.

THE DEAFENING NOISE inside Bolero's pulsed with too much bass. Garmon had invested a small fortune in the sound system and not much else in his effort to renovate and reopen yet another disco. Anna hated this kind of club. The music wasn't to her taste, the place was dimly lit to hide the shabbiness, and Ray always parked her at a greasy table, and took off with one or more of his cronies, leaving her to nurse one drink for long enough for it to be embarrassing. If she wanted another, she'd have to pay for it herself. It was shaping up to be another one of those evenings already and she was fighting a headache. The steak was turning in her stomach.

Having a flashy broad on his arm went predictably in Ray's favor with the mutts he ran with. Middle-management gangsters as far as Anna could tell. The less attention she paid the better. There would be no more readings tonight. She was sick from it, body and soul, yet she knew Ray would badger her for information that she didn't have.

She took comfort in knowing that by the time they got home, the last thing on Ray's mind would be sex. The ground rules had been in place for a long time, even before she'd gone away to school. The few times that he had tried to have sex with her, he couldn't get it up, and, in his anger and embarrassment, had blamed her and even hit her once in frustration.

She threatened to leave him, but he begged in a pathetic, tearful spectacle, even threatening to kill himself. Now she wished she'd said, "Do it, Ray, do it," and handed him a razor or poison. Anything to get the job done.

After that, he stopped trying and she was fine with it. She would play the girlfriend, but he had to leave her alone. He'd have to solve his problem on his own without her help. Day by day, they would keep each other's secrets.

It all boiled down in the end to not being alone and not having a plan, but she kept telling herself that it was different for her. That she needed to mark time. Staying with Ray was keeping her out of the game that everyone else was playing with wild abandon, the game of life.

She wanted something more than partying and dumb rutting until she tricked some fool into thinking he was in love, marrying him and then living off him the rest of her life. Ending up as someone's legal property. She wanted more, but what, she still couldn't say. No, staying put would do, for now, until she was ready.

But that was all about to change.

ONE HOUR, twenty-five minutes, and four assholes asking her to dance later, Ray came out of the VIP room still head-to-head with Bruno, the club manager. Bruno, who was raving and waving his cigar around. Ray was chattering in his ear like an ape. The two of them coked to the gills. Anna stood up, her disgust with Ray and anger with herself making her sick to her stomach.

"Ray, we need to get going, you know, you have that other thing, in Bridgeport?" Anna said.

Ray looked at her stupidly for a moment, then put on a long-suffering face and turned to Bruno.

"Yeah, she's right. We gotta hit the road." Bruno was too busy leering at Anna to come up with a suitable protest right away.

Then Bruno beamed. "Well, my man, why don't you go ahead and take care of your business and leave the lady here with me? I could show her a good time."

She wouldn't put it past Ray to do just that. Without comment, Anna turned on her heel and headed for the door leaving Ray to grovel and apologize to Bruno for her attitude.

"Woman needs one upside the head," Bruno advised. Ray agreed with a grunt.

Anna hurried out the front door to the side parking lot and leaned on the fender of Ray's mother's Cadillac. The headache had bloomed into a full-blown migraine, and she bent over and vomited violently next to the car, the strawberry daiquiri and her dinner looking like so much lumpy, black blood on the pavement in the shadows. She wiped her mouth with the hem of her dress, took deep breaths of the damp night air, and tipped her head back trying to stop the roaring in her ears. It started to rain lightly, and she stepped closer to the building hoping for some shelter. *Where the fuck was Ray?*

From the deep shadows behind her, a man stepped up and took her firmly by the arm.

"Hey honey, had a little too much to drink, did we?"

She reeled and tried to break his grip but didn't scream. It would have hurt too much to scream. The cheap uniform shirt said that he was one of the off-duty cops Garmon hired as security, but there was no professional deference or concern in the way he gripped her arm. That grip went from cruel to painful the second it became clear she was going to fight him.

"Bitches should never fight," he growled, "especially drunk bitches in their fucking high heels." He twisted her off balance and she staggered against him.

"Let go of me, you motherfucker!"

"And a dirty mouth, too. I like that, sweetheart. Who left you all alone out here looking like this?" He squeezed her breast like he was testing melons in the produce section. Anna slapped his face hard as Ray finally came around the corner jerking on his ridiculous driving gloves.

"Get off her you cocksucker" he yelled, but he hung back a few seconds watching how he'd like to handle her himself, appreciating the arch of her back as she struggled against the painful hold on her arm. The guard was twisting her arm and lifting her, making her breasts strain against the dress.

Ray shook himself out of his coke-fueled reverie and fumbled a knife out of his pocket, nearly dropping it because he was unprepared for the force of the spring-loaded blade. Pie-faced and bug-eyed, he postured foolishly, holding the glittering knife out with his elbow high like a bullfighter. He was still too far away from the action to injure anyone but himself. Everything shimmered in the mist falling through the single arc light at the far corner of the lot.

Anna staggered on her heels and the man eased his grip on her, lowering her to the wet pavement while reaching slowly behind his back for the gun in his waistband. Ray closed a step, the blade flashed. She knew how sharp it was– she'd sharpened it herself, hoping Ray would cut himself. The sound of the bass came through the walls of the building and clouded the air around them.

The man let go of her altogether and she crouched below the action as he grinned and showed Ray the snub-nosed, nickel-plated gun. Just a handful of death. Ray dropped the knife to the wet pavement right next to her and stepped back, both hands splayed out in front of him, terror on his face. She was invisible. The man with the gun laughed.

Time slowed to a crawl. The light reflecting from the raindrops strobed and wrapped around her, the noise from inside the club pulsed inside her head. Suddenly, the air turned cold, and snowflakes spiraled around them, rising instead of falling. What followed came back as a dream that Ray corroborated the next day.

For the men, the moment flashed deadly. Anna picked up the knife left-handed and stabbed the man in the gut, chest, neck, and face as she rose to her feet. Four sure, power-backed sticks, each hilt deep, as if the blade were hot and he was made of butter. The gun clattered to the pavement, and she was showered with blood as he collapsed, boneless. The snow turned back to mist.

Ray shrieked once like a woman. Anna collapsed across the dead man, blood in the whites of her eyes. Ray looked around furtively and pocketed the gun. He unlocked the Caddy and hauled Anna like a bloody sack of potatoes through the back door, depositing her on the carpeted floor. He went back to the dead man and grimaced as he pulled the knife from the victim's right eye and dropped it in the car by Anna's feet. Another quick look around and he rolled the body back into the shadow of the building.

Shaking all over with a combination of fear and fury, he got the car started, turning the key a second time, making the starter screech, then lurched it out of the lot, checking the rear view obsessively until he nearly clipped a guardrail.

She stuck that pig like it was nothing! For what? Some minor insult? My mother will kill me if anything happens to this fucking car. I'll have to clean up the blood myself. Bitch!

His guts cramped, and fearing he might shit himself, he pulled violently off the road into a gas station parking lot, flung the car door open, and sprinted for what he prayed was an unlocked restroom. Anna was sprawled across the floor, the bloody knife at her feet.

Ray stood in front of the filthy sink, splashed water on his face, looked himself in the eye and smiled—something he didn't do very often—but while he was hunkered down on the crapper, he thought about how he had a murder weapon covered with the victim's blood and Anna's fingerprints.

WITHIN THE WEEK, Anna and Ray were standing before a rum-soaked justice of the peace somewhere in Jersey. An old woman with her hair in curlers stood squinting through her cigarette smoke as a witness. For twenty bucks and their signatures, they were married in less than ten minutes. There were no flowers, no rings. No one objected as Ray scrawled the bride's name on the paper because she was barely sober enough to stand, much less sign her name. Anna couldn't remember saying "I do". Ray dropped her off at Angel's Rest and disappeared for the weekend. Nothing— and everything—was different.

~O~

S1:E19

Anna always arrived early. It gave her time to settle in, clear her mind, and check the surroundings for potential troublemakers. The mall was nearly deserted. None of the restaurants served breakfast and the handful of people scattered at the sticky tables in the atrium were employees waiting for places to open, hunched over sacks and cups from fast-food joints. The air smelled of burnt coffee and bacon grease. She was going to have to look for another place to give readings. This one was getting depressing.

She sat in the far corner of the open area where she could watch people coming and going, her back to the wall like an old-time gambler. The client had agreed on the first time and place that Anna suggested, tipping her off to the urgency of the woman's need for answers. There was a clock ticking somewhere in the lady's life.

Head down, lost in thought and anxiety, Mrs. Gill was easy to spot as she made her way across the food court. She had been Anna's Lit teacher in junior high. She'd grown a little bit frumpy looking in nine years. As she sat down, Anna got her first shock of the morning. Now, in her late thirties, Mrs. Gill was pregnant, and it was getting harder every day to keep her secret. Her morning sickness was intense enough to make Anna vaguely nauseous, nevertheless, Anna smiled a welcome. Barbara Gill only managed a tight grimace as she pulled up the chair. Anna got right to it.

"Let's skip the pleasantries and take a few seconds inside ourselves. Just close your eyes and think about where you are in your life right now and what it is you need to know." The routine kept small talk to a minimum and gave her the opening she needed to do a quick read of the client so she could put together a meaningful reading no matter what cards turned up. The second shock of the morning made Anna take a long breath and sit back in her chair, a furrow between her eyebrows.

Usually, her client's concerns were as boring and mundane as the local paper. "Is my husband cheating on me?" or "Should I quit this fucking job?" She only gave them just enough to keep them coming back. Anna had agreed to a last-minute reading for an anonymous client only because one of her regulars had begged her. 'A friend of a friend' situations were always dicey and this one would be the mother of no exceptions.

She shuffled the cards quietly and placed the deck on the table between them, leaving her hand over the deck as she took a quick look around. The last thing she wanted was a crowd. "Go on and cut," Anna urged.

Barbara Gill was busy picking her cuticles bloody. "Like this?" As if doing it some other way would change things.

"Any way you want," Anna said. "It's all about your energy." This much she believed. Anna respected the imagery and history of the Tarot, but it was her ability to know a client's history for the reading that she used. She was just going through the motions because the moment the woman sat across from her, Anna knew the full scope of her problem—Mrs. G had been having an affair with one of her students. He was a senior now, headed for college around her due date in the fall. He didn't know.

They had been extremely discreet; no one—not even his best friend—knew. There was no doubt the child was his. She and her husband had given up trying to conceive years ago; sex with him had become a routinely bitter pill. Now she was faced with a decision that would not only affect her life, but the lives of her lover, her husband, and her child, forever.

Anna laid out a cross of six cards, two at the crux, and a line of four beside it—the Celtic cross. The size and complexity of the layout gave her a lot of cards to work with, plenty of wiggle room, but she wanted to help, to make a difference. It was unusual that she even cared enough to have an opinion, but Mrs. Gill had respected her in class, been kind even, and Anna had a terrible feeling she might do something desperate, something foolish. This time the reading wasn't about the money.

Without specifics, Anna called the cards as she turned them face up. The Empress turned up early, a card signifying fecundity and creation. Opposing it, the Three of Swords—loss, and sorrow; The Wheel of Life was for changes; A Knight was a young lover, and the Emperor, the husband. *Perfect, perfect.* And finally, most significantly, Justice—a decision had to be made and soon. There were other cards, but these were the ones that mattered. Anna wanted to be kind, but she was starting to register rising anger from the woman across from her.

"Cut the crap," Barbara Gill said impatiently. "You're not telling me anything I don't already know."

Anna knew she was dying for a cigarette but was working hard on quitting her pack-a-day habit. She tapped her finger on Justice. "Are you asking the cards to make *this* decision for you?"

Barbara didn't answer but crossed her arms over her chest defensively; she was warring with herself.

Anna gathered up all the cards except the ones on the staff–the outcome of the reading. The Wheel of Fortune was at the bottom of the staff. It wasn't significant in this reading, but visually impressive. Anna put her closed fist on it, knuckles down, and said, "It's time to stop being a coward."

"How dare you!" Barbara fell back on their old teacher-student relationship, but times had changed.

"Shh!" Anna hissed, looking around furtively. "I'll tell you how I dare." Anna lowered her voice even further. "You've already decided to keep the baby and tell your husband that it's his. He'll believe it only if you never, ever tell your lover the truth. You must break it off with him completely and let him live his life. You're halfway home. This child will be your salvation. She deliberately held back that she knew Barbara's lover was one of her students. She didn't want to scare her any further. "Do you want to know if it's a boy or a girl?"

Mrs. G. sat back in her chair, the blusher on her cheeks floating on her shocked pallor. Anna was glad that she was more angry than frightened, but worried that the woman might start to cry. The last thing Anna wanted to do was touch her by way of comfort knowing the contact would make her puke.

The older woman looked away from the table, mouth set, her tired eyes fixed on some point in the future. After a moment, she got up without a word and walked away leaving a crisp, folded fifty on the table. Anna sighed, picked up the money, and fished around in her purse for a piece of gum. She was still queasy and relieved this was the only business she'd scheduled for the day.

~O~

S1:E20

When Anna got back to the apartment there was a business card tucked blank side out under the dented brass number nailed to the apartment door. She took it down and scanned the message scrawled in red ball-point pen under the printed "Lt. Daniel Delgado, Boston, First District" and a series of printed phone numbers that had been crossed out. Under these, he'd written a local number and 'call me'.

What was he doing here and why did he want to speak with her? She had an instant physical reaction that was so conflicted she could only giggle at the chill on her neck and shoulders the same moment as her pussy clenched and tingled. She remembered his fine face and how small her hand felt in his when they'd said goodbye in the hospital courtyard.

Ray jerked the door open startling her. He snatched the card from her fingers and held it out of her reach.

"I guess he figured I wouldn't tell you he was here, the prick. I saw him pull up and park, but I didn't answer the door." He read the message and said, "Smooth operator. I knew he'd be checking up on you one way or another." He tucked the card into his shirt pocket.

She said nothing and walked past him, but her heart was skipping like a needle on an old forty-five. The sad kindness in Delgado's eyes. The warmth and linger of his handshake. God, she was so easily amused these days. What was wrong with her? She knew the answer: starvation of the heart.

RAY FOLLOWED her into the kitchen yammering on. "I suppose you should meet with him, but the damn investigation was closed, over with, so what's he doing here? Have you been in touch with him?" With this last question, he grabbed her by the arm.

"Cut it out," Anna said and jerked away from him. "No, I haven't, and I have no idea why he wants to talk to me." *Oh yes, I do.* The only time Ray ever paid her any attention was when some other man noticed her. He went straight for the nasty. It wasn't love.

"Of all people to be looking at you twice, a cop. Just what I need." He slammed the refrigerator door. They were out of beer.

"That's right, Ray, it's all about you. Maybe he took a shine to you up in Boston and calling on me is just an excuse to pitch a bone to see if you're a catcher." Without warning, he slapped her face.

Anna turned her back on him, knowing that was as far as he would go if she didn't fight back. She could feel the striped impressions of his fingers rising on her cheek and forced herself to action so she wouldn't cry.

As if she was getting first aid for someone else, she jerked open the freezer, took out a bag of frozen peas, and pressed it to her face. She had to be in court in the morning and wouldn't be able to cover up the marks if she didn't act quickly. She was sick to her stomach and appalled that she knew these things and acted on them without thinking.

Without apology, Ray said, "Call him and set up a meeting and we'll put this shit to rest."

DANIEL DELGADO WAS WAITING for them at Beaker's the next evening. Anna hadn't been there in years. She liked the dark, coziness of it, a lover's meeting place. As she made her way through the tables, she made eye contact with him but watched his happiness falter at the sight of Ray right on her tail, all puffed up and ready for a fight.

She had the fleeting impression that he was a reader, but it passed. He was just good at his job. Very good. His disappointment at seeing her with Ray confirmed for her that his main reason for getting in touch was personal. Her pussy had been right.

Daniel stood, but didn't put out his hand. "Good to see you both again. Anna, you're looking well. Please, have a seat."

Still the same self-absorbed asshole he'd been when he met with the police in Boston, Ray glowered with thinly veiled hostility, "What's this all about, Lieutenant? I thought the case was closed."

"Yes, you're right, it was." Daniel assured him. The waitress interrupted them, dropping three menus on the tabletop.

Ray put them back in her hands. "We aren't staying. What is it, Detective?"

Anna kept her eyes on Daniel's hands, long fingered and graceful. She imagined he played a musical instrument. Then she reached for his thoughts with an invitation. *Here.*

Tomorrow at four. Daniel paused, momentarily distracted, but then he smiled and nodded.

"Yes. Yes," Daniel repeated, distractedly. Another pause, and then, back on track. "The case is officially closed, but it's protocol to let all the victims in the cases that I've worked on in the past two years know that I've transferred to the NYPD and will no longer be their main point of contact in Boston."

"You could have put that in a letter."

"Yes, of course, but I've relocated here, and it wasn't hard to find you both. I hope you don't mind."

Anna smiled. She still hadn't spoken a word beyond a murmured hello. He was faster on his feet with the bullshit shovel than she was, very charming indeed, and she was pretty sure he got her message.

Ray stood up, practically lifting Anna out of her seat. Daniel searched her face for traces of fear or alarm. She seemed serene, composed. Still disarmingly attractive.

Ray said, "Well, if that's all, we'll be leaving."

Anna leaned across the table and took Daniel's left hand in hers. "Thank you so much for everything you've done." *Here, tomorrow at four.*

He stood and said, "Thank you both for coming." and remained standing as Ray steered Anna ahead of him out the door.

THE NEXT AFTERNOON Daniel was sitting at the same table, a mixture of surprise and pleasure spreading across his face as she headed his way. He rose to greet her. "I don't know if it was my idea or wishful thinking, but I'm glad I decided to come back. Will you stay and have something? A drink?" The same waitress loomed with her pad and pencil.

One look at him and Anna's plans shifted. He was even

better looking than she remembered. Still the jacket and tie, but jeans now. He commanded his space with his size and restrained gestures. His dark eyes were intense but full of humor. Hair, shiny clean, and recently styled. A whiff of a green-note aftershave made her mouth water. For a moment, she forgot what she was going to say.

"Just coffee, thanks." She had to find out if there was anything more to his interest in her—if he still associated her with the unsolved case.

"You'll have to excuse my husband. He's kind of old fashioned. He'd have a fit if he knew I was here now, but I needed to apologize and explain."

Daniel looked like a man who'd just stepped off a curb. "Husband? I didn't know you'd married. I kind of hoped…"

She didn't let him twist. "I know, Daniel, that's why I came."

"I don't understand."

"To make sure you understood that I'm not available."

He looked down at the tabletop. At first, she thought he was embarrassed, and she was sorry she'd put him in the position. Then he surprised her.

"Funny that you said available instead of interested." Daniel reached across the table and slipped his hand under hers, resting his thumb over the place on her finger where a wedding band should be. She didn't flinch or try to pull away. "Let's just say I'm not all that convinced."

She didn't need to read him to know his disappointment and she had to check her own sadness at this missed opportunity. She couldn't risk leading him on. Her heart, but mostly her freedom could be at stake. Boston had been one thing. The incident at the Bolero was something else. Ray had warned her that he'd rat on her if she tried to leave him. Not trusting herself to speak, she drew her hand away from his and twisted her coffee cup in a slow rotation.

He sat back in the booth and said, "Well, we could just stay in touch then. Can't have too many friends, right?"

His smile still heated up her heart and she felt her resolve to let him go get wispy and full of options. *He's right. Friends in high places. Friends who could make things happen. Get away with things, even.*

"I'd like that." She nodded. "Everyone needs friends."

~O~

S1:E21

So much for the lunch crowd. They were more work than they were worth. I finished wiping down the tables and bar and was just about to go back to my newspaper when she came in looking like she'd just stepped out of a forty's movie. What did my wife call that kind of dress? A sheath, like a cover on a knife, fitted close, everything covered, yet nothing concealed. Black. Cadillac black. Even her hair and makeup had a forties feel. She was that kind of blond that's half sun-bleached and half attitude; you know she's darker down below, but somehow that's so right.

I could tell she wasn't a woman who expected attention for her looks. She was not in style, but style had gone begging in the face of classic beauty, the place where she lived and thought nothing about. We were either in a time warp or there was a costume party warming up somewhere. She wasn't even carrying a purse. I wondered what the sob story would be, but no matter what she wanted from me—time, money, blood—I knew I'd give it up and wish I was twenty years younger.

Her eyes met mine. I asked, "What can I do for you?" not

"What can I get for you?" or more properly "Can I see some ID please?" I wanted to step into the dangerous play she had just swept into the room. Someone was in for it.

She put her hands on the bar, ring-less, dagger-tipped fingers spread like stars, and said, "An old-fashioned glass." Like she was going to tell me how to cast a spell. I was already in, ready to take any direction, and reached under the bar where I'd hidden a pair of Waterford crystal glasses I'd picked up at a flea market not long ago. Now I know why I hadn't brought them in the house. The red paper napkin on the bar and her lipstick were a match, the heavy glass centered on it, glittering, waiting for those lips.

She said, "Three ice cubes, two slices of lime, squeezed, and some cherries." Wordlessly, I built the potion, waiting to see where she was going with it. She paused and looked over my shoulder at the top shelf. I was getting lost in her eyes and had to blink. Then she surprised me.

"Three fingers of Beam and a splash of soda."

I thought, *Can I name this after you?* From nowhere, she put a warmed ten on the bar and chuckled, low and musical, as if in answer to my unspoken question. She took two deep sips and closed her eyes. The liquor took her coloring up a notch immediately, lips, cheeks; her eyes bloomed from gray to deep blue. In the movie, she'd take a cigarette out of her bag, and I'd hold the match for her. No such luck.

A man paused in the doorway blocking the glare from the street. I watched her face change as she looked at his reflection in the mirrors behind me. My fantasies were tattered cobwebs in the slight breeze he let in. He took the seat beside her, leaned his forearms on the bar, and asked for a draft beer. He was more of the here and now type— tan, longish hair, sideburns. The not-quite drug dealer look the young men all cultivated, but a little better dressed in slacks and a dress shirt open at the collar. Odd and slightly out of place for broad daylight in the middle of the week. Like her.

There was no greeting, no conversation at all beyond what went on between the mirrors and their eyes. She lifted her glass and knocked back the drink like a sailor and then stabbed up a cherry and a piece of lime with the straw and ate them slowly. He tilted his head to watch this exhibition, for it was a show put on just for his benefit, even though I was standing there polishing a glass. If they weren't already acquainted, they soon would be.

He picked up his mug and finished it in one long go, setting it back down on the bar. I caught his eye to see if another beer was in order, but no, there was something else lined up.

He said to her softly, "You go ahead."

I have a good ear for accents; he was a long way from Boston. She slipped out of the chair, stood tall next to him, and smoothed that black dress down over her hips and ass. He and I had a few seconds of brotherhood as we watched her walk across the floor to the jukebox, something about a racehorse in her stroll. That may seem like a crude comparison, but I happen to think thoroughbreds are beautiful animals. No matter what's happening up front, there's just no hurrying the back end. Did I mention her ass? Or those fucking high heels?

He took a bill from a steel clip, but I held up my hand to say, "On me." He nodded once and headed her way, checking the room as he went. The place was empty. That's when I made him for a cop.

She was somebody and he was there to look out for her, or so I thought until they stood side by side in front of the juke and she snaked an arm around his waist. He brought some change up from his pocket and fed the machine while she punched the buttons. The music and the magic started at the same time.

The first song caught me by surprise. The bar owner was a sentimental old fool and kept the juke filled with all kinds of music. It was something from the sixties with a cha-cha tangled in it, "Johnny Angel". I wondered if he was a Johnny. They danced like a couple from American Bandstand, loose and sweet. She made a mistake and he gently corrected her, and he tightened his lead. The man was in charge. Or so I thought.

Each time he took his eyes off her, his gaze swept the room. Now I was sure he was a cop, undercover too, by the look of him. "On the Street Where You Live" by the King of Cool himself was next. Ladies first, so that had to have been his pick. What in the world were these two going to do with a song that was popular when they were in the cradle if even born?

She was a much better dancer than the first song let on. He was sure and debonair, but he was singing the words to her, for her. His heart was in her hands, poor bastard. They were tight, like this was something they wanted, but couldn't have. I thought about the painful box step my wife forced me into for our wedding reception. This was something else.

The last song started, and the lights should have dimmed. It was Lenny Welch teaching us about heartbreak with "Since I Fell for You". So that was their story. He took to the baseline and held her close, but I could feel that she was leading this time, schooling him. Taking it all back in spades.

Bodies close, they held each other's eyes, foreheads touching. The building could have burned down, and they wouldn't have known. Hands that had been white-glove proper were now tucked between them, connecting hearts. Her free hand was on the back of his neck, fingers cradling his skull. His left hand had drifted from her back to her waist and now cupped one perfect globe of her ass. I imagined they could fuck standing up and realized I was sweating. I wished my wife were here so I could show her what was still possible.

The song ended and, rather than the intimate display I was expecting, he rested his lips between her eyes a moment, she whispered something, and he nodded in response. When she lifted her chin and smiled at him, something glittered on her cheek. She straightened up, took a deep breath, and headed my way. I made a lame pretense of being busy.

She looked at her change on the bar but made no move to pick it up. "I'd like to thank you," she paused and looked back across the room, "for the hospitality."

"My pleasure," I said, and meant it. She turned to go—there was that glitter on her cheek again—and was out the door in six steps. I counted them. I heard an engine start, a big block muscle car, and something black and chrome rolled past the front door.

He was leaning against the wall by the juke, arms folded over his chest, studying the floor. After a minute of deep silence, he came back to the bar where I'd set out another draft. He looked at it but didn't sit down.

I've never been one of those world-weary bartenders who held themselves up as the guy with all the answers. Far from it. My natural response to most questions is the slow negative—lips sealed with a touch of *What are you gonna do?* from my shoulders. Cowardly, I know, but I got my own problems. This was different. I gave him an opening.

"Looks like you got a problem."

He blinked and came back to the moment, knocked back half the draft, set it down and said, "She's married."

I didn't have an opinion about that. A lot of people get married wrong, but I pressed, even though I know I shouldn't. "Divorce?"

"It's complicated."

In other words, "Shut up", but I remembered the tear on her cheek and couldn't leave it alone. "You're on the job, right?" I had to know if my instincts were still working. He looked at me and then himself in the mirror.

"Yeah, there's that too," Boston cop confirmed. I waited.

"So?" The unspoken question, *what are you going to do about it?*

He picked up the mug, drained it, and put a bill on the bar. He seemed to have come to a conclusion. He put his sunglasses back on, got up, and said, "You never asked, and I never said." And he was gone.

~O~

S1:E22

J ack got off the train and made his way to the cavernous main concourse of Grand Central Station. He didn't walk; he bopped. When he was on a mission, the music in his head had no off switch. Nothing made him feel safer and more anonymous than zigzagging his way through the swarms of people milling there, each with a purpose and each unknown to all the rest. It was like wading into the river Jordan and coming out clean in the 42nd Street waiting room.

He checked the clock and the departure board for the next northbound train and picked up his pace. As he passed through the waiting room to the street exit, he saw Walter out of the corner of his eye; black baseball cap with white, stick-on letters that were never the same twice. Today the cap read T M D. He'd asked Walt about the letters once and instead of an explanation, got an icy glare and that all-too-familiar ache in his fillings. End of discussion.

Still mulling over the letters on Walt's cap, Jack stood on the sidewalk halfway up the block waiting for the next bus. Walt was down the line behind him as the bus wheezed and leaned into the stop and they boarded. Jack dropped into a seat as the bus lurched away from the curb and everyone still standing staggered for a handhold. A stout woman in a frumpy suit dropped down next to him. She smelled like mothballs and Jack's eyes started to water. Out of boredom more than suspicion, he checked her out and his stomach knotted and rolled.

Not every Void needed God's judgment delivered by Jack; some only hated and abused themselves and recoiled at the idea of interfering with anyone else, but, to some of them, animals were fair game. This one passed her weekends feeding poisoned popcorn to squirrels and pigeons all over the city. As sick as it was, there were those who would pay her to keep it up. The inside of her head felt like a basket of hot snakes and Jack slapped himself mentally for being nosy, yet again. Sometimes all they needed was a nudge from him to alter their course, but he was too invested in this transaction with Walt to take the time. He didn't much give a shit about pigeons either. *Jesus, roll me a joint.*

Dipping into people's heads was how Jack made his way in the world. If he was sober, all he had to do was focus on the person to get a clear picture of their state of mind and what they were planning. Proximity improved the read, but he always kept a safe distance in case further action was warranted. He counted on the element of surprise and had mastered the art of being unobtrusive.

The worst Voids were not compulsive. They were planners, stalking their victims, imagining the moment, and plotting all the moves necessary to make their kills. It seemed Jack couldn't ride the bus or subway without bumping into someone who needed bumping off. Add in the cokeheads and the city was becoming a circus of venality. It exhausted him. Since he'd started selling upstate, he'd noticed that troublemakers were rare in the country, and he looked forward to the weekends to get away from the crowds.

Three stops later, Mothball Lady heaved herself up and got off. Walt slipped into her seat, nodding perfunctorily at Jack. They each carried thick, manila interoffice envelopes, ubiquitous on the city streets, each with columns of blacked out or stickered over names and addresses, the red waxed strings secured around cardboard buttons.

Jack shifted his envelope to his left armpit as the woman got up to leave, and as Walt took her place, they each dropped their envelopes to the seat between them. Walt stood up just as the bus rolled to the next stop, Jack's envelope in hand. He got off and met Jack's eyes through the window from the sidewalk for the briefest of seconds, slipped on his sunglasses and, with Jack's envelope tucked under his arm, crossed the street behind the bus. "Slick as snot" Gordy would say.

Jack lifted Walt's envelope, hefted it once. Pot was heavier than cash. He waited a stop, jumped off the bus and raised a fist to flag a cab. Whooping bursts of sirens echoed up and down the block as two police motorcycles bulled their way through the crowded street making way for marked cars. Traffic came to a standstill.

The next train back to Brewster left in fifteen minutes and now Jack would have to double-time it. He was going to cross the street to avoid what appeared to be a crime scene. Rather than be seen skirting an active criminal investigation with a pound of weed in his possession, he hugged the building and joined the rest of the looky-loos craning their necks to see what or who, had gone down.

At first, all he could see were dark shoes and khaki-clad

legs. He ducked and got a glimpse of a dark baseball cap with white letters and Walt's waxy face with a pool of blood under his head, as a yellow plastic sheet was pulled over him. He hadn't seen a bullet wound which meant that Walt never saw it coming. The envelope with the cash was gone. Jack was glad he and Walt had no kind of relationship beyond business. Was Walt even his real name? There would be a lot of fingerprints on that cash, but none of them Jack's.

He stood up and casually walked the last block back to the 42nd Street station. By his watch, he had come out this way only twenty-two minutes earlier, Walt right behind him, walking, talking, living life with no clue that his time was almost up. There would be repercussions, but who knew what they might be. It wasn't as if Jack had gotten the weed for free.

The conductor bellowed "Board!" just as Jack ran flat-footed down the ramp to Track 49. He slipped into the last car and made his way forward to the smoker, but when he got there, it was packed. There were men and a few women already waiting for seats in the thick blue air; the windows were brown with nicotine. Just being in the car for a few minutes was enough to take the edge off.

He made his way through the smoker to the next car and took an empty seat as the conductor approached him for his ticket. Jack pulled it from his back pocket and smiled as the conductor punched it and tucked it into his pouch, touched his cap, and made his way to the front of the car. Jack was just about to relax into the ride when he noticed the conductor lean in and speak to a man with a crew cut sitting at the front of the car. There was something about their body language, the conference held a beat too long, the slightest turn of the man's head; Jack bolted from his seat and made his way back through the crowded smoking car.

He didn't have to get into either of their heads to know the crew cut was a cop. The train clanked and shuddered as it pulled away from the 125th Street station, and at the last sane second, Jack jumped from the metal steps to the platform dashing down the stairs, vaulting over the railing to the street, and hitting the ground running. From the busy sidewalk across from the platform, Jack could see the conductor and the plainclothes cop still struggling through the crowded smoking car as the train picked up speed.

~O~

S1:E23

J ack ducked into a bodega halfway down the block, greeted the man behind the counter by name, and stepped into the old-fashioned phone booth tucked in the back corner of the store. He pulled the screeching door closed, slid the fat envelope into the slot where a phone book used to go and called Gordy. The end of the envelope with the button and string stuck out. He picked at the tape over the button idly while the distant phone rang.

All this fuss over a pound of weed. Was there no real crime in Manhattan anymore? Walt's death and the bullshit on the train confirmed his decision to get out of the business. More and more, the risks were outweighing the profits. The thought of a weed peddler needing a lawyer on retainer was ridiculous. People just didn't know how to have fun anymore and Jack was all out of get-out-of-jail-free cards. Gordy finally picked up.

"Hey, I'm gonna need a ride," Jack said. "It got hot on the train."

"Shit, I won't be down there before, six-thirty, seven."

"S'ok. Pick me up at the church."

Gordy knew he meant Holy Spirit in the Bronx. Jack was going home.

HE PUT the phone back on the hook and someone tried to open the folding glass door which jammed against his boot. A lithe, brown hand tipped with blood-red fingernails snaked through the small opening and caressed his face.

"Jacky. Let me in. It's Essy."

Jack smiled and moved his foot out of the way, and she skinned through the opening and dropped into his lap. Estrellita lived on the top floor of the building across the street. She used to be one of his regular customers until Hector warned him about selling in his neighborhood.

"So, what do you have for me Jacky?" she purred and crept her fingers under the bib of his overalls, scratched his bare chest lightly, wriggling her tight little ass in his lap.

"Essy, you know I'm not doing business here anymore. I promised Hector I'd sell no weed on his block and he promised to not break my legs, you know?" He bounced her on his knees. "I like my legs. You like my legs, right?" They had danced together at Connie's studio when she had the neighbors in for rent parties. Essy was a terrible dancer, but she was fun to watch.

She piled on the drama. "Oh, Jacky. I'm so disappointed." She buried her pretty face in his shoulder and pretended to snivel and he got a face full of spring-loaded, black curls all stiff with hair spray. Abruptly, she stopped the fake boohooing, looked him in the eye and said, "What if, what if you didn't sell me any pot, but we traded for it, eh?" She let her hand drift down to his crotch. Jack tipped his head back and made a show of grimacing thoughtfully.

"Hector didn't say anything about trading, did he?" she purred, stroking him through the thin denim.

"Well. No. He specifically said selling now that you mention it. Essy, you should think about going to law school, you know?"

Essy stood up and they traded places, Jack with his back to the glass door, hands on the back wall of the booth while she sat on the curved metal seat and unbuttoned his fly. He lifted the envelope out of the slot and pressed it against the phone booth wall with one hand – it would not be good to forget and leave it behind.

"Jacky, you know how I hate these stupid overalls" she fussed. He slipped a slim baggie of pot out of the chest pocket and tucked it into her cleavage.

"I wasn't thinking about you when I got dressed this morning," he said into her hair.

Jesus. I hope nobody calls this number. He lifted the receiver off the hook and laid it across the top of the box. He had been on his way to the church and now he lifted his St. Christopher medal and held it between his lips while Essy gave him a blowjob. Father Ramos always told the boys in Sunday school to give ten seconds of prayer to the Holy Father in Rome before committing a sin. He gave another few minutes to Hector's baby sister Estrellita and her fire-engine red lipstick.

JACK BOUGHT a package of Twinkies and a single Heineken and hit the street, the envelope tucked under his arm. He hadn't gotten out from under the bodega's tattered awning when Hector pulled his overwrought lime green Olds convertible to the curb in a cloud of blue smoke. The car needed engine work and Hector spent good money on whitewall tires. Jack held the sweating bottle of beer to his crotch to cover a wet spot and squatted down beside the car, hanging on to the door handle. He gave Hector a quick read to gauge his mood. Although they had been friends since elementary school, Hector took his machismo a little too seriously and was quick to get physical if provoked.

He's been given a bump and he's happy as a pig in shit! I can screw with him.

"Hector!"

"Jack! My man! Long time no see! What're you doing in the neighborhood? Not business I hope." He thumped his hairy fist on the car door for emphasis.

"Hector, would I go back on my word? I'm not selling anything, in fact, I'm giving away free samples!"

Hector frowned. "Samples of what?"

"Sperm samples. I just left a load with your Mama!"

Hector blinked and then bellowed laughter. "I got no comeback man. It's been a long day. You need a lift?" He reached out and plucked one of the Twinkies from the open pack and stuffed it into his mouth whole. Jack did the same with the remaining one, washed it down with a sip of beer and said, "Yeah, drop me off at Holy Spirit?"

"You got it, my man."

AS JACK STOOD up to go around and get in the passenger side, Estrellita came out of the bodega with a bag of potato chips in her hand. She stood there sullenly eating the chips, knowing what was coming.

"Estrellita!" Hector barked, "How many times do I gotta tell you about coming out of the house dressed like that? You look like a slut!"

Jack hooked his thumbs into his overalls and looked

down at the sidewalk. Essy crossed behind him out of Hector's view and patted Jack's ass. As she took off running down the block, she flipped her brother the finger. They both watched her ass as she fled.

"How old is she now?" Jack asked as he climbed in and pulled the door shut.

"Hey man, that's my sister you're talking about," Hector warned.

"Never mind then. Let's get back to your Mama!" Jack punched him in the shoulder.

They both convulsed with laughter as Hector launched the car into the stream of traffic heading across town. They were still laughing and had gone only a few blocks when the great sloping windshield of the Olds shattered and caved in on them in a shower of broken glass. Hector screamed, clutched his head, and stomped his foot to the floor on the gas pedal. The seatback gave way and he fell back flat. Jack grabbed for the steering wheel as the heavy car slewed forward and scraped the mirrors and door handles off a dozen parked cars as they careened down the street.

"Get off the gas," Jack yelled, and the rear window exploded. Someone was shooting at them. Jack kicked Hector's foot off the gas and stomped on the brake bringing the car to a screeching halt. The car that had been tailing them slammed into the rear of the heavy Olds. Jack was thrown against the dash, Hector popped up into a sitting position, blood streaming between his fingers. He yelled, "GO! GO!" and stepped on the gas again.

Jack steered them down the one-way street and turned into the first side street that was clear of traffic. The other car did not follow. Hector let off on the gas and the Olds lurched over the curb up onto the sidewalk. Jack was afraid to look at him, but Hector struggled into a sitting position and said, "Dude ... my fucking white walls! Did you have to hit the curb?"

Hector had a dark furrow running across his forehead and the blood oozing from it had painted his whole face. Jack couldn't tell if the wound was from the flying glass or a bullet.

"Never mind the wheels, I think you need a hospital."

"Fuck that shit. Give me that." Hector snatched Jack's bandanna off his head and pulled it down over his cut, retying it tighter. "Now, find me something to prop this fucking seat up so I can drive this bitch out of here."

"Who's mad at you Hector?"

"Who is mad at me? Who is mad at you gringo?"

"Come on, everybody knows your car."

"That's right! Everybody knows me, knows my ride, and until ten minutes ago when you got in that seat, nobody in their right mind would fuck with me, so Jack, you see the problem?"

Jack flashed back to Walt lying on the pavement, his life leaking away. The less Hector knew about that, the better for everybody.

Hector pounded on the blood-spattered steering wheel. "Whatever the fuck shit you've stepped into is on my floor mats now. I need to find out who the fuck and deal with these assholes."

They stuffed an empty trash can in the back seat to prop the driver's seat upright. Hector wiped the blood off his face and looked at his hand. He banged his fist on the outside of the door again. "Some motherfucker gonna wish they done this right. You coming?"

Jack stepped back and shook his head. He couldn't wait to get on the train back up to Westchester. He didn't have the stomach for this relentless wild west shit anymore.

"No thanks, I'll get a cab." He shook shards of broken glass out of his hair.

"You won't get one up in here. Get in an I'll get you out to the avenue. Then you need to get the hell outta Dodge, amigo, and don't forget that." He nodded at Jack's envelope on the dash. It was speckled with broken glass and fresh blood.

~O~

It had been a week of non-stop action, most of it handing off customers to the competition. Deals, parties, meet and greets with sketchy strangers, and now, this bullshit ride through the barrio with Hector. *Fuckin' gunplay? Seriously?* Jack was hungover, hungry, and exhausted mentally, spiritually, and physically. Confession would be good for something if nothing more than killing a little time before Gord picked him up, but he wouldn't go to Holy Spirit.

The priests and nuns there might have known him best at one time, but the church put him out just when he was beginning to understand his place in that world, and he still held a grudge. And so, he had Hector drop him off a block away from Sacred Heart, one of the most beautiful cathedrals in the city. He hoped the doors weren't locked. They were all dark inside these days, budgets cut to the bone.

He slipped into the confessional and let the cool calm seep into him. In some way, the church always welcomed him back. It was the people of the church who were a thorny pain in the ass. The priest slid back the little window.

Jack mumbled, "Bless me, Father, for I have sinned. My last confession was, um, six months ago."

There was a pause and the priest prompted him, but Jack's burnt-out state had left him wide open; on full receive. Jack got the full force of the fear, anxiety, and self-loathing coming off the man on the other side of the screen like a bucket of cold water full of fist-sized ice cubes.

Jack felt himself studied, examined, and rejected, too old for the young priest's perverted taste. With his first words, the depth of Jack's voice had made it clear that he was not the fifth-grade truant or runaway the man might have longed for at this time of day. Jack leaned away from the screen and squeezed his eyes shut, but it was too late to stop that first-time reel. Most people have a first time they never forget. Jack's first kill parked his heart and opened the door to his future.

JACK AND A FRIEND from elementary school were supposed to be getting ready to serve Mass. He and Andy had been buds since the two of them went on a successful shoplifting spree in third grade. The priest, Father Dennis, he wanted to be called, was new. Jack was late and blundered noisily into the closet-like locker space that the altar boys shared.

Something was wrong with Andy. He looked seasick, sitting on the bench with a grubby surplice hanging from his hands. The heartsick grief and disgust came off his friend like the smell of a dead dog. Worse, Andy's thoughts of suicide made Jack's heart squeeze up into his throat. *Jesus! Yeah, you! Why here of all places?*

Jack took the cheap lace smock from him. "Stay here."

The priest's office was two doors down the hall. Jack found Father Dennis bent over in an armchair beside the unused fireplace, tying his shoelaces. Without looking up, Father Dennis had said, "I'll be right there Andy."

With the surplice wrapped over his hands, Jack lifted the heavy brass poker from the hearth and, with an overhead swing that would have rung the bell at Coney Island, buried the hook and point deep into the molester's skull. He unlocked the door to the alley, left it ajar, and ran back to Andy.

"Call the fucking police. Somebody's killed Father Dennis!"

JESUS! Yeah, you! Why here of all places?

But Jack already knew the answer. This was where they preyed on the innocent. The priest cleared his throat. He must have asked Jack what sins he wanted to confess, but Jack wasn't listening. This priest was new, from somewhere in the Midwest. In the last couple weeks, he'd already claimed a victim; a ten-year-old, a doe-eyed little Mexican boy whose parents were now punishing him for wetting the bed that he shared with his two younger brothers.

"What sins are you confessing?" the priest repeated.

"My sins?" Jack fell back into the present and repeated hoarsely, "My sins?" There was a roaring sound in his head like a hurricane making landfall. He stepped out of the confessional and looked around. The sanctuary was empty, the air dead.

Jack took a knife from his pocket, opened it with a flick of his wrist, and stepped into the priest's side of the box. "Don't scream and I won't hurt you," he lied, grabbing the priest by the front of his shirt jerking him up and out of the box. Jack hustled him out the side door to a narrow, windowless alley. He held the point of the blade under the white notch of the Roman collar at an angle so the man could see the knife. At first, he resisted, and Jack yanked him upright and scraped the knife along his jawline. The priest looked into Jack's passionless dark eyes and thought he knew what was happening.

"Are you the Archangel?"

"Sure, whatever you say. Get down." Jack forced him to his knees. His palms pressed to the stones, the priest leaned his forehead against the cathedral's cool granite skin and began to sob.

"Mother Mary, pray for us..."

"Shut up." Jack kneed him in the back.

"You know about my boys don't you."

"They were never yours," Jack hissed into his ear.

"Will you hear my confession?" the priest whined.

"No."

"Will I be forgiven?"

Jack paused long enough to be sure that his answer would sink in. "No."

He held the man's head against the wall with one hand, seated the edge of the blade under his ear, then pulled it across his neck above the Adam's apple, digging deep, feeling the edge grind against gristle and bone. Ear to ear, he followed through with a high-held flourish, then wiped the flat of the blade on the priest's black wool sleeve.

Blood sprayed against the wall, ran down the rough-hewn granite and puddled at the priest's knees. His hands slipped from the stones to his sides, and he sputtered, whether it was from the wound or his mouth, Jack couldn't tell. Jack forced the man's head hard against the wall until the bleeding slowed to a stop. Two minutes? Three? The noise inside his head had stopped, at least. It would echo for a while he knew. A garbage truck rumbled past the mouth of the alley, followed closely by a car, horn blaring.

Jack took the dead man by one arm and dragged him to the rear of the alley to an open dumpster. He pulled the body upright against it and boosted it over the lip of the chest-high metal box letting the body slide over and in soundlessly. There were half a dozen bags of trash piled against the outside of the dumpster and Jack dropped them over the corpse.

A five-gallon pail of water swarming with wriggling larvae sat beside the dumpster. Jack held the knife by the end of the cheap, wooden handle with two fingers, swished it once, then dried it on his pants leg. One just like it could be bought or stolen from any bodega on any block, but he'd honed the razor-sharp, six-inch blade to deadly and was fond of its utilitarian heft. There was a spot of blood on his right thumb, but he was not about to put his hands in that water.

He closed the knife, pocketed it, then took the bucket back down the alley and tipped the contents over the blood on the wall. The green-brown water followed the rivulet of the priest's blood to a storm grate set into the concrete. Five filthy gallons were enough.

Jack slipped back through the side door, retrieved his envelope from the confessional, and made his way through the sanctuary. Normally, he would have stopped in front of the altar and genuflected. This time, he kept walking through the nave to the front door. The vast room was still empty and hollow. No one was home.

He paused at the ornate marble font, looked at his reflection in the holy water and washed the blood from his hand. As an afterthought, he splashed his face and blessed himself. Who else would do it?

Hope had been lounging across the pew closest to the confessionals intent on overhearing the salacious details of Jack's sinning. The brazenness of these Papists never ceased to amaze her. The entire notion of sin and repentance seemed a grand sham to her. What happened this time stunned and frightened her. What kind of man was Jack, if he was a man at all, and once again she wondered why she had been assigned to him and felt fear. *Lord Jesus, are you sure he's one of yours?*

She stood shivering by the font after Jack finished there, looked down into the water, then slipped into the street behind him, a watery edge to his shadow.

He headed down University Avenue toward Holy Spirit. This spontaneous killing had shaken him. He usually planned his actions, nothing left to chance. Jack thought back to the girl in the park. The little librarian. Again, spur of the moment. That killing was haunting him. This one wouldn't scab over any time soon.

In the past, he'd be well on his way to wasted at a party somewhere, history up in smoke. Now he was mulling things over, second-guessing himself. A real confession would have to wait until he could get to St. Bridget's and Father McLeod. A change of scenery couldn't come soon enough, but Chang had warned him, "It's only geography, Jack."

~O~

S1:E25

Anna woke gasping in the stale air of the Falcon. She'd ransacked the apartment in vain, then fallen asleep lying across the front seat of the old car, the contents of the glove box, even the ashtray, dumped on the floor. No real help anywhere. The half joint in the ashes on the floor would be good for an hour if she didn't have to interact with anyone. A wave of nausea forced her out of the car. It was happening fast. Her body was trying to turn itself inside out.

On her knees in front of the toilet, she couldn't stand up the spasms were so violent. Between retches, she spit into the bowl smugly thinking how other women might be worried about being knocked up. This was no immaculate conception, just bad judgment, letting the overlapping layers of prescription drugs spin out of her system at the same time.

The physical symptoms would pass in a few days if she took nothing. An easy dry-out some might say, but mentally, she was naked. Exposed to whatever emotions people dragged around with them; the fear, misery, guilt, and hatred that people poisoned themselves with, moment to moment, Anna was wide open to all of it without the drugs. The effects of weed or alcohol were too fleeting for her to consider them any more than just entertainment, and tomorrow she was facing a court assignment and some readings at a party that she'd already been paid for. High or drunk wouldn't help, and there was no backing out. This was her livelihood at stake.

The day before, she'd taken the last Valium from the unlabeled bottle always in her bag and didn't think much about it. There were prescription bottles all over the apartment—black beauties, reds, yellow jackets, white crosses—Ray was a recklessly indiscriminate abuser. An ever more frantic search found all of them empty. She slammed the medicine cabinet door and spoke to her reflection in the cloudy mirror.

"What kind of evil motherfucker puts an empty pill bottle back on the shelf?"

Five bottles, to be exact, all of them crowded to the back of the sticky glass ledge hidden by a jar of Vicks, eyewash, Pepto, and an empty bottle of cough medicine. He was even drinking that now. Ray had been helping himself to her favorites for weeks, the ones she took to survive long periods of close contact with other people. Even her stash of mixed pills in the nightstand was missing.

Anna staggered to her feet and washed her face with cold water, then bent and drank from the flow. Her skin was splotchy, eyes red-rimmed. She couldn't bear the thought of going into the ER at this hour and making up some bullshit, much less submit to being examined. In the kitchen, she poured cold black coffee into a cup and spilled a bottle of aspirin onto the counter. Three chased by the muddy brew and she caved. There was only one speedy solution, and it was just a phone call away.

"Jesus, woman, it's the middle of the night. You sound like a junkie."

"It's medicine Bobby and I'm out. Are you going to help me or not?"

"Where's Ray? He owes me money."

"I have no idea."

"My old lady is going to kill me if I leave."

"I have cash, Bobby. Do you keep your balls in the sock drawer? Tell her it's business then go back to bed."

"Park in the garage by the elevator. I'll be the asshole in striped pajamas."

WHAT WAS NORMALLY a twenty-minute drive took forty. Every cop in the county was out on patrol. Shift change. As long as she minded the speed limit, no one looked at the Falcon twice. She pulled into the underground garage, got out, and walked into the dim stairwell. Light from the top of the flight spilled down weakly, illuminating the half-open elevator door. No Bobby. Everything smelled like piss.

She headed back out to the car. "Where are you, asshole?" The lighting in the garage was just as dim, less than half the bulbs in steel cages working. She tripped over something and went sprawling to the filthy concrete. It was Bobby, lying on his side between two cars, his greying hair matted into a gash on his head. Blood trickled down his face into one eye. His pajama shirt was ripped open, pants pockets yanked out.

She was late and he'd waited, the drugs stashed somewhere close. Smooth Bobby only delivered after he'd counted the cash. They beat him because he was empty-handed, and they were too stupid or desperate to believe what he told them. Footsteps and voices scuffled closer. To her relief and horror, he groaned. Anna whispered, "Play dead, stupid."

She backed into the shadows, up against a concrete pillar as Bobby's assailants cursed, trying and kicking car doors just rows away. The weak beams of two flashlights flitted everywhere, bouncing off chrome, dying in the pipes and wires of the ceiling. She sidled along the wall trying for deeper darkness. Instead, she found herself in a corner.

Something rolled in the grit underfoot, staggering her to a crouch where she found a two-foot length of rusty rebar. Long enough to whip and heavy enough to maim, she clutched it like hope and groped her way back along the damp wall away from the trap.

There was a gap between two massive concrete pillars. She reached in to feel if it was a passage or a dead end and raked her fingernails on the rough surface. Not two feet deep. The flashlight beams washed across the littered floor, and she backed into the tight space, holding the rod overhead, the rough surface of the concrete snagging her sweats at the hips and elbow. The first one to come within reach would be the first to die.

"Motherfucker! It has to be here somewhere."

"We'd be gone already if you hadn't hit him, you stupid fuck. Shut up and keep looking."

The two men were working their way through the row of cars parked closest to the stairwell, groping bumpers, checking behind tires. Her car, keys still hanging in the ignition, would be the last in line. If they started it, the headlights would point right into her hiding place.

SHADOWING her since she got out of her car, Sam wrapped his arms around her as she crowded back into him as deep as she could into the gap, cobwebs breaking in her hair, sticking to the sides of her face. She closed her eyes and took a shaking breath, willing herself to not panic. Warmth seeped into her from behind, as if the wall had been baking in the sun. She leaned into it and the sound of her heart hammering in her throat, the sounds of the frantic scavenging and cursing, receded. Slowly, she brought her arms down in front of her, flexed her shoulders, and adjusted her grip on the rebar. The heat gathered in her throat and flowed down her spine, like hot syrup through her heart, and into the pit of her stomach. Like a double dose kicking in, the pain in her bones softened, spread, and melted away. She licked her lips, squeezed her breasts together with her elbows, and gave the rebar a practice flail.

Sam spread his hands over her hips, pulling her back against him tighter even as she leaned into the danger. As a weakening beam of light wobbled her way, the building's air handlers activated, and a huge fan set into the ceiling came alive with a rumble and squeal of rusted metal sending cobwebs and trash flapping and skittering. Moisture in the air crystallized and danced on the frigid blast through the searchers' errant beams of light. Flecks of what felt like snow curled into her refuge, melting instantly on her burning cheeks.

A caged light bulb swelled from yellow to white and popped, sparks and shattered glass raining down on the men. In the space of a few seconds, all the other bulbs burst plunging the garage into total darkness. The air handler quit suddenly with a metallic clang. A flashlight squelched out and hit the floor. She could see the street. A car passed by in the cold rain.

"That's it. Fuck this shit. I'm outta here," one of the voices hissed.

"Fuck." The stumbling footfalls and arguing receded. A car door slammed out on the street. She never saw their faces. Two of the overhead lights sputtered back on.

Mouth open, panting, Anna slumped back into Sam's fading grasp, her legs crossed tight. The heat and tension that had been gathering in the pit of her stomach and crotch fluttered like a bird at a windowpane and flew away. "Oh, my fucking goddess," she moaned. "What the hell was that?

A voice from the shadows answered. "That was me almost getting killed." Bobby was sitting up, his back against a tire as he wiped blood from his face with his sleeve.

"Jesus, Bobby, are you okay?" Anna stumbled out of her hiding place, dropping the rebar with a clang.

He touched at his scalp gingerly. "It's not that bad, but if my wife comes down here and sees you, she's gonna finish the job. Help me up." She helped him limp to the car parked nearest the stairwell. He leaned against the tired-looking station wagon. "I guess it was good that you were late. Where's the cash?"

"Um, they didn't get the goods?" Anna pulled the money from her cleavage.

The folded bills were sweaty, and Bobby took them from her like he was handling a dead rat. He opened the gas cap door, pulled out a baggie of blue pills, and handed them to her. "Those are tens, so watch yourself. And don't tell Ray where you got 'em."

She moved to embrace him, but he held up a blood-smeared hand. "Get out of here before you get me killed for real."

. . .

S<small>AM TOOK THE PASSENGER SEAT</small>, *hanging on to the dash and door handle, his ears still red. He shifted from one ass-cheek to the other as if he were sitting on pins and needles.*

"That's some hot business you conducting, Sam." Hope knelt in the back and hung over the seat between him and Anna, her chin on her folded hands. She grimaced as Anna dry swallowed one of the blue pills.

"I don't know what you're referring to," Sam muttered.

Hope snickered. "Right. I never seen a woman get so close just from a hug from behind. You must talk some sweet line of trash, country boy."

The red of Sam's ears flashed across his face in a deepening blush. "She put herself in mortal danger thinking she could fend off those highwaymen alone."

"But you woulda handled that for her just like before. No, I'm talking about the way you heated her up, made her wet." She reached around and brushed Sam's hair out of his eyes with a cool fingertip. He pulled away from her touch, the muscles of his jaws clenched.

"Good. You keep up that holy Joe stuff, cause their paths are about to cross, then we get to watch." Hope punched Sam on the shoulder. "Don't you growl at me, son. She ain't for you."

~O~

S1:E26

"Louie!" the pimply kid yelled over his shoulder. "Guy here to see you."

The kid peeled off his dirty apron, shot Jack a furtive look, and hurried out the front door slamming it behind him. Louie emerged from the back room, his face at first guarded, then astonished.

"Holy fucking shit! Jack!" Louie bustled from behind the counter, locked the glass door, flipped the 'open' sign to 'closed', and turned off the neons. "You look like a goddamn narc!" The last time he'd seen him, the boy's brown locks were shoulder length. Lou reached out to tousle Jack's hair, now a ragged, uneven haystack, but Jack grimaced and stopped him with a fierce grip on Lou's wrist. Jack didn't like to be touched casually.

Lou gave him space. "You grew."

Jack looked at their reflections in the glass. "They say that shit happens as time goes by." He was taller than Louie now. The traces of the last regulation haircut long gone; his hair had grown like weeds—trailing, wild, defying gravity.

He pulled a baseball cap from his back pocket and snugged it, brim low.

Since he'd been discharged, Jack had been working part-time for Chang's Moving and Storage company in the day, a few evenings at Connie's, and moving weed after dark.

Chang's sons, Go and Chi, were behemoths. Six-two, two-ten apiece, they took turns breaking Jack's balls by giving him heavy boxes to carry while they handled the furniture at four and five-floor walk-up jobs. Jack figured he'd been lifting and carrying more than the two of them put together and it showed. Without asking, the Navy and the work had wrapped twenty pounds of muscle to his not quite six-foot frame. Connie was pissed that none of the dress clothes she had kept for him at the studio fit anymore, but she let him work in jeans and a t-shirt and the ladies loved it. He kept himself busy, laying low, assessing the changes that had come over people and places while he was away.

Lou spread his hands wide on the counter. "So, what do you got for me?"

Jack worked a flat package from the liner in the back of his jacket and dropped it on the counter. Lou hefted it once and stowed it out of sight.

Jack took a piece of bubble gum from the plastic tub on the counter, unwrapped it and said, "Same service, same rules. Speed called you?"

"Yeah, this morning. He starts his day by giving me agita," Lou muttered. "What the fuck? A two hundred dollar jump in one week?

Jack shrugged. "Flux in the market, my man. You heard about the half-ton the feds snatched off the Jersey Turnpike the other night? Supply and demand."

Louie handed Jack an envelope. "Count it," he grumbled. "My customers are not going to be happy."

Jack snapped a pink bubble. "Send them to Jersey. See how they like the price of fun over there."

The older man grunted. "Speaking of demand, when are you gonna bring me some blow? It's starting to feel like an outpost of Woodstock up here."

"Sorry, Dude," Jack lied. "I don't think Speed trusts me that much."

He didn't tell Louie that he'd refused a second package, one that Speed wanted delivered to an address on the Upper West Side. The dealer had dropped the too-solid package on the coffee shop table with a thud. Jack just looked at it, fists in his pockets.

"I told you I won't be handling your snow bunnies." Jack didn't say why and the long, bored look that Speed gave him let Jack know that Speed didn't care why. His frustration with Jack was festering to an end. A sale should have been a sale, but Jack knew that coke customers were unpredictable and toxic to him in ways he couldn't talk about.

As cocaine was taking the city by storm, Jack had concluded that he was allergic to it. There was no high for him, no buzz, just an aggressive anxiety, a sore throat, and a headache. The third and last time he tried it, he got into a fistfight at a wake and woke up in an alley behind the funeral home in a puddle of piss that he wasn't even sure was his. The fact that he couldn't read coke users was irrelevant - there was nothing useful going on in their heads anyway.

An elderly woman crept up to the register. Jack had seen her coming, but Lou jumped and said, "Jesus Christ, Stella, you give me a fucking heart attack. I forgot you was in here. One a dese nights I'm gonna lock your ass in."

She had an armload of groceries and dumped every-thing onto the counter. Three different kinds of cookies, a bag of marshmallows, Cheetos, and a quart of A&W root beer.

Stella was seventy if she was a day. She wore a blue turban, big sunglasses with green lenses, and a red quilted satin coat buttoned from her chin almost to the floor. Dirty pink ballet slippers. Maybe five feet tall, she looked like a displaced dignitary from a very foreign country.

"You got the munchies, Stella?" Lou said, looking at her selections.

"Never you mind, Mr. Capella, just ring me up so I can get on with it."

"Eighteen-fifty."

Jack eased off the counter, pretending to read a comic book. The old woman reached into a black leather fanny pack wrapped twice around her tiny frame, extracted a hundred-dollar bill, and passed it to Louie. Her hand hung in the air for a second, then, with a sharp fingernail, she poked a hole in the plastic window of a box of Entenmann's with a loud pop. She tweezed two cookies out. "Cookies gentlemen?" Lou made a face and shook his head no.

"Don't mind if I do." Jack plucked them from her finger-tips and popped them into his mouth whole.

She looked at him over her sunglasses and hissed, "Gonif." He winked back.

Lou peered over her head. "Stella, where the hell is your cart?"

She looked around vaguely, then at the pile of snacks, and muttered, "Oh, fuck."

Jack bent double with laughter, choking on cookie crumbs. He had idly tried to read her, but as Lou suspected, she was as high as a kite and walled off from Jack's mental intrusion. Despite her buzz she'd seemed in command of herself until now.

"Okey-doke." Lou pointed at Jack. 'Robbing the Hood' here is going to carry your shit home for you, aren't you, Robin?" Before Jack could say no, Lou put the paper bag in his arms. "It's all of three blocks, dude. See the lady home. Stella, don't forget your change."

She took the cash from him, folded the bills carefully, and worked them into Jack's back pocket.

"Home, Robin," she said imperiously. Lou unlocked the door, let them out, flipped the sign to "Open", and turned the neons back on.

THE ENTRANCE to the unprepossessing building was set back from the street behind a locked metal gate and an over-grown courtyard. There were no names or numbers over any of the polished brass mailboxes in the foyer except one. Number Six. Jack said, "Do you live here alone?"

Stella eyed him a moment. "Yes, I do, and if you murder me and stuff my body down the garbage chute you'll be on candid camera. Lou will rat you out to the cops and I will haunt your hippy ass."

"Good to know," Jack said, looking around the lobby over the bag of groceries for a camera. "Maybe I shoulda shaved."

He thought he knew prewar brownstones, but this one took him by surprise. Its inner opulence wasn't evident from the street. The parquet floors of the small lobby gleamed under a dimmed crystal chandelier. Stella opened the wrought iron gate to a tiny elevator.

Jack hesitated. "I'll take the stairs."

The door to her apartment was open. Light spilled out

into the dark hallway where her grocery cart stood shiny sentinel just outside the elevator. Jack paused in the hallway to hack, catch his breath and curse cigarettes.

Despite her years, Stella was on the ball. "I take it that Louie calling you 'Robbing the Hood' would be a reference to the dramatic increase in how he is ripping me off for pot?"

Jack almost choked on his bubblegum and decided the only way forward with Stella would be the unvarnished truth. She waved him into the galley-like kitchen; plenty of room to work, but nowhere to sit.

"And the quality lately. Disgusting. If I didn't know better, I'd think he was growing it in rat shit in the alley."

"I won't apologize for other assholes, but I've been out of the supply chain for a while and Louie is a greedy…" Jack groped for the right word, mindful of the company.

"Motherfucker!" shouted Stella, her arm in the air like Lady Liberty.

There was nothing funnier than old people getting high and acting up and Jack was again convulsed with laughter.

"Hear, hear," he coughed, tears in his eyes.

Stella opened the box of Entenmann's properly, stuffed two cookies in her mouth, gestured to the refrigerator and said, "Get milk and glasses and come with me."

He followed her down a dark hallway that was lined floor to ceiling with framed paintings and photos. Except for the tiny kitchen, the entire apartment was wall to wall and floor to ceiling with paintings, drawings, and photographs. The frames ranged from starkly contemporary to gilded rococo. Here and there, he thought he recognized an artist's style, but not the piece itself.

The large front room faced Central Park. If you could ignore the city skyline in the distance, the view looked how he imagined an English countryside might look. The only furniture in the room was a large dining room table big enough to seat twelve, the kind with carved, hairy legs and feet. There were only two armchairs. Half the massive table was heaped with books, magazines, file folders and newspapers. Apparently, Stella did not entertain.

Stella took a plain white tablecloth from the back of one of the chairs, snapped it briskly into place over the cleared end of the table, and gestured for Jack to take a seat. He poured milk for two and sat back in the chair looking at the painting that occupied most of the wall facing him. It was a huge welter of ribbons and splats of colors that looked like the artist robbed an Earl Scheib paint and body shop.

Stella looked around the room as if to find the thread of activity she'd momentarily displaced, slapped her hands together and said, "I'll be right back" and disappeared down a darkened hallway.

Jack got up to get a closer look at the other art. Spotlighted on the rear wall was a life-sized portrait of a man and a woman. The costumes set the painting sometime in the twenties. The man wore a dark, severely cut suit, a gold watch chain looped across the vest, the stark white collar a glowing slash at his throat. Thirty-ish, tall and lean, his dark, slicked-back hair and clean-shaven face spoke of a man who wanted to be taken seriously, but the trace of a wry smile said that he took everything with a grain of salt, even his own self-importance. His hands told more.

Hanging loose by his side, the left hand curled into a casual fist that promised power. His right rested possessively on the place where the woman's long neck curved into her shoulder, fitted there like he was giving her life.

The woman sat on a low stool, leaning back against him, her head against his hip intimately. Heavy-lidded eyes devoured the viewer, daring anyone to judge her, lips glistening and slightly parted. The dress was transparent layers of cloth paler than her pink skin, crisscrossed over small breasts. There was an illusion of nipples. The cloth wrapped her body and legs like a winding sheet then exploded in a froth of ruffles at her feet. Her short, dark gold hair was arranged in waves but was slightly mussed. Although carefully posed, they were far from perfect. There was a mystery between them as dark as the black background they dominated.

Jack stepped in close and studied their faces and said to no one, "Looks like they were just screwing."

From right behind him, Stella said, "We were."

"Jesus Christ. Louie was right," Jack exclaimed, clutching his chest. "You'll give a guy a heart attack." She crept around the room like a house cat. Invisible until she pounced. She dropped a little wooden box onto the table, opened it and pulled out a wrinkled plastic bag filled with what he assumed was pot.

"I paid him fifty dollars for this shit just last week."

Jack opened the bag and sniffed. It was skunk weed at best, tainted with something unidentifiable. He wouldn't smoke it.

"Awright. Dump it down the crapper. You don't buy from Louie anymore and if he says anything about it to you, tell him you got Jesus and he can go fuck himself." Jack had no doubt that Stella would quote him. "I'll take care of you." How much pot could one little old lady smoke? He took a slim joint out of his pack of Marlboros. "Here, save this for later and if you like it, I'll bring you an ounce. Wholesale."

Stella took a gold lighter out of the box. "No time like the present. Step outside. Shouldn't smoke around the paintings my lawyer tells me."

There was a terrace off the kitchen. He could see she probably spent a lot of time out there. A jungle of potted plants on wheels massed in one corner. A dirty teacup, ashtrays, a rain-swollen paperback with the cover gone, and a pair of high-powered binoculars in a waterproof case lay on the table between two wrought iron chairs. From his seat, Jack could see into the dining room where the massive painting was quietly rioting on the wall.

Stella lit the joint, took a deep hit and asked, "Do you like the Pollock?"

Jack shrugged. "It's okay to visit but I don't think I could live with it. Are you sure it's real?" He'd heard Chang talking about a Pollock forgery scam as if he'd dodged a bullet.

Stella looked at the painting a minute. "Oh, it's real enough. I bought it from him cheap before everyone decided he was the cat's pajamas." She blew out a thin cloud of smoke and added, "He was a mean drunk and a bum lay."

Jack coughed on laughter. "Thanks for reminding me my generation didn't invent partying."

"You got that right, young man."

It was the other painting that had gotten Jack's attention. The artist had captured something larger than the two people on the canvas. He wanted to know more about them, but it seemed too personal to ask.

It was getting late. The city was in full spangle across the deep darkness of the park and Jack was thinking about where he'd be spending the night. The Navy had coughed him up months ago and he still hadn't bothered to find a place. He'd pick up a girl, spend a night or two, and then move on before the web got stickier. Martina in Chelsea had left phone messages in three places since he'd been with her last week. Three too many. The couch at Go and Chi's pad was passable but staying with them was predicated on getting up at six in the morning and putting in ten hours of hard labor. They worked like the devil was their landlord and so far, Jack had no idea what they did for fun. He was ready for a day off. Nobody would miss him.

"Stella. Now that you know all my business, can I crash on a couch here tonight?"

She considered for a moment. "There's a guest room at the end of the hall. You can help yourself to whatever's in the closet, although I doubt there will be much to your taste."

Jack said. "I'm easy. Thanks."

"Never mind thanks. You'll earn it."

The room was clean and spare, the furniture solid, and the shower hot. After months of couches, futons, and sleeping bags, the bed felt like heaven. On the wall opposite the bed, another large abstract painting glowed in the city light that filtered through the blinds. Blocks of dark colors, blue and purple, floated on a rich golden background in the manner of Rothko. He fell into bed grateful and slept like the dead.

It was still dark when he woke. The building was unnaturally quiet for Manhattan.

Thirsty, he walked down the hallway to the kitchen and stood in the open refrigerator door, naked, drinking milk from the container, surveying the rest of the contents. A middle-aged woman tying a crisp white apron over a dark dress came into the kitchen from the other direction. She looked him up and down, lips pressed together hard against grinning.

"The glasses are over the sink. She's already outside on the terrace waiting for you. Put on some clothes."

Jack slunk down the hall knowing she was watching his retreat. He came back in jeans and a dark linen shirt from the closet. The woman handed him a tray of fresh fruit, muffins, and glasses of juice. "I suppose you live for coffee?"

"If it's no trouble. Ma'am."

She searched Jack's face and said, "Careful with her this morning. She's not having a good day."

"What gives?"

A sad, distant look crossed her face. "She called me 'girl'. She mighta done that in another life, but never to me in this one. Not in the thirty years I been working for her." She shook her head sadly. "The doctor said there could be some meanness with the pain." Then she looked at him fiercely. "Been a long time since she let any you boy toys stay over." Jack started to protest, but she laughed and waved him off. "Yeah, yeah. You men think you the only ones with longings, but you hurt her or take advantage, and I'll throw your sorry ass off the balcony. Coffee will be a minute."

"Yes, ma'am." He thought better of saying anything else and took the tray outside to face the dawn breaking over Manhattan.

BUNDLED IN HER QUILTED COAT, Stella sat on the table, binoculars to her eyes. He put the tray down beside her and started in on an English muffin. After a minute she said, "Oh my," and handed him the glasses. "Third building from the corner. Blue umbrella over a picnic table. Big balconies they got over there."

Jack trained his sights on the building and saw the umbrella she was talking about. Then he saw the naked man standing in the open doorway just beyond it.

"What a specimen," she cackled.

Jack put down the glasses. "You're a piece of work, Stella.

You couldn't find a naked woman for me to eyeball before coffee?"

She rubbed her dry palms together briskly and said, "I'm sure you find your share. Break out another number, would you, Jack? My bones are trying to kill me today."

Jack already knew. He'd read her while she was still surveying her domain and he heard and felt the sound of someone hanging up. Not an angry slam or a sly return of receiver to cradle. A hang-up. The undeniable click that signaled life's end. He'd only heard it a few times in sober memory, but each time the truth of what he'd experienced had been borne out by a death. There was no unhearing it and he'd never told a living soul.

He was sorry Stella wouldn't see summer again. He'd felt her pain first, distant, like a dial tone running through his bones. Her bones. Wrapped around that hum, something else he couldn't place. A longing that wasn't sadness because the end was a given and beyond that end, something wonderful. Was she a believer? He hoped so.

She plucked at the collar of the dark blue linen shirt he'd pulled from the closet. "Nice choice." She nodded. "Thomas, my second husband, had all his clothes custom made. Everything in that closet came from a Hong Kong tailor downtown that he kept secret. Drove all his cronies crazy that he didn't run off to London for his clothes like they did, and he always looked the sharpest."

"Is that the guy in the painting?"

"No. That was my first husband, Carlo."

Jack waited for her to continue, but she had gone still, drawn in on herself. Jack threw her a line. "How long were you and Carlo married?"

She looked up from her wizened fingers. "We had three

grand years together. From the day we met until the day he didn't come home."

"What happened?"

She shrugged. "I never found out. The people he did business with, his business, was...shady. Criminals. I think he trusted the wrong person."

The maid brought the coffee and Stella changed the subject abruptly. "So, what do you think, Em, should we keep him? He can get all those boxes and crates out of the way on the ground floor."

Emma eyed him suspiciously. "Do we have to feed him too?"

Jack had an apple clenched in his teeth and was peeling the paper panties off a huge blueberry muffin. He looked at Em and winked.

Stella said, "You won't have to complain about food going to waste anymore." The woman sniffed and left them alone.

"I could use a place to lay low for a while. What do you need done?"

"Just getting rid of stuff. The building is full of it. Loose ends."

Jack nodded and pulled a joint from his pack of Marlboros. He lit it and passed it to Stella, but instead of taking it from him, she unfolded her legs slowly and leaned over to climb down off the table. Reaching out to steady herself, she planted her hand on Jack's shoulder, her dry fingers touching his neck. He saw the contact coming and steeled himself to not flinch from her touch.

The connection came so hard and fast that he couldn't move to break it. If she'd meant him harm, he'd already be dead. The images, impressions, and emotions of how it had been between Stella and Carlo blew through him like a freight train. From the acute intensity of the sex to the heart punishing sugar-rush of love, and the hopeless desolation when it was over, he felt all of it the way she had lived it, three years' worth in less than ten seconds. He felt like he was falling and couldn't even tense his muscles, his reflexes paralyzed.

Feet finally on the terrace, Stella lifted her hand from his shoulder and patted him on the head like he was a good dog. She stepped to the railing and went back to scanning the buildings on the west side of the park where the sunrise was painting them pink. Jack thought she was oblivious to what had just happened, but she said, "You're not the only one, you know."

Still shaken, Jack sipped his coffee and said, "What are you talking about?"

SHE LOWERED the glasses and searched his face. His eyes were the same warm brown as Carlo's, but young. Untroubled. "Carlo was like you." She took another hit from the joint, passed it back to him, holding her breath briefly. "We feel it, you know. Most people don't know what's going on when the likes of you pry into our thoughts, but we feel… invaded. I know because Carlo told me everything. Too much."

Jack didn't reply and looked over the edge of the balcony at the overgrown chaos of the courtyard six floors down. Something was stalking something down there, the moving grasses, betraying the progress of the hunt. One person talking did not make a conversation, so he let her talk.

"I think someone scared you into solitary. Just like Carlo was when I first met him. It doesn't have to stay that way, you know. Don't be alone, Jack." She smiled out at the view.

"She's out there somewhere. You'll know when you find her. Believe it when you do."

Jack looked out across daybreak on the city. "You make more of me than there is Stella, but thanks for the concern."

JACK WAS GIVEN KEYS. Nights he didn't come home no one mentioned it. He conducted his business and kept it to himself. He imagined he could see the spot where the girl had died through the trees from Stella's balcony. The story about her murder evaporated. There was no mention of the dead priest in the papers. For all Jack knew, his body was rotting in a landfill, the man's absence noted, but unremarkable. The deaths shook him in ways that had never happened before. The feeling that he was shoveling shit against a fierce tide grew.

THEY WATCHED TV. Baseball, old movies. Soaps and Soul Train. Smoked a lot of pot. Played gin rummy. He rearranged the art, Stella working him like a film director. She had pieces from many important artists of the twentieth century. Early works she had purchased cheaply. The Pollock. A series of Picasso watercolors. In the spare bedroom, the Rothko. There were more in crates on the other floor. A museum's worth of art.

Em was a great cook and showed off for Jack. Stella's appetite picked up a bit. Em joined them at the table for dinner but left in a cab after Jack cleared the dishes. Stella got worse by small degrees but never complained. Soon, Em came to stay. There were more pills now, and a doctor came to the house. Real house calls.

March slipped into April like the morphine in Stella's IV.

Jack had a delivery down in the village with plans to stay on for the party. He left Stella and Em with beer, pizzas, and pastries that he'd brought from Arthur Ave. The doctor was on call.

It was well after two when he crept back into the apartment. He had trouble focusing on whoever was trying to wake him not long after. It was Em. He could tell she had been crying, but that she was finished with it.

"She's gone, Jack. Slipped away in her sleep, sly girl. I need you to come sit with her. I have things she wanted done and she shouldn't be left alone. Not yet."

Jack sat in the high-backed armchair by the bed. Stella could have been sleeping. In recent afternoons, he'd sat reading the paper to her, stopping when he thought she'd drifted off. She would snap her eyes open and say, "And?" and he would finish the article.

Now he watched her face for long minutes expecting that 'and?' any moment. It didn't come and soon he slumped back in the chair and slept, his bare feet up on the bed frame. Jack dreamed.

Two ELDERLY WOMEN were playing cards in a dimly lit room. Dirty crystal ashtrays and glasses with golden liquid caught lamplight and lit the lined faces that were by turn, bemused and intent. The old nun rocked in her chair to knock back a brandy. She pulled one card from the deck on the green cloth and said, "After all he's seen, he's still the Page of Cups with a heart full of wild." She crossed herself. "I warned him from the cradle. Never tell, Jack. Never tip your hand and never dare love."

The other woman was Stella, her white hair like a halo of horns. She drew three cards and lay down two. "Wrong again," she cackled. "You don't have all the answers, Sister."

The old nun snatched up another card, tucked it into her hand and countered, "Nothing changes. We'll always be hunted. Burned or hung."

Stella waited, tapping a yellowed fingernail on the green cloth. "You takes, you gotta put, them's the rules."

The old nun frowned and discarded one card.

Stella snatched it up triumphantly and shouted, "Gin!" She held the card up and then reverently spread out her winning hand. "Finding the right one changes everything for all of us." Crowned in glory and robed in mystery, the Queen of Hearts glowed on the field of green felt between them.

EM TOUCHED him on the shoulder gently as the sun warmed the curtains. He woke up with the taste of brandy in his mouth and the smell of popcorn in his nose. He hated popcorn. In basic training, a guy who had flunked out of pre-med told him phantom smells and tastes were a serious thing. "It's probably a brain tumor. Get your shit in order, man."

But Jack didn't buy into it. The dream, though. *What the fuck was that about?* Stella was still dead. By noon that day, her body had been taken away.

Em had a to-do list for him. Rooms on the lower floors to be unlocked. Calls to be made. Workers to be let in and watched.

She said, "Take what clothes you want before they come." People from a homeless shelter were coming for everything in the refrigerator, pantry, and closets. A team of workers was cataloging and crating all the artwork, books, and papers. A lawyer and his assistant walked around with clipboards overseeing everything while Jack and Em mostly stayed out of the way. The whole operation went off with military precision. Jack waited for the locksmith while Em took a stack of mail to the post office.

Stella not only had all her ducks in a row, but she'd also schooled them to shame the Rockettes.

There were no callers. There would be no funeral. A day later, the building was locked up and Jack was out on the sidewalk with his duffel bag. All the trees in Central Park bloomed at the same time and the pollen count was off the charts.

~O~

The argument in the living room that dragged her from sleep was getting louder. All she wanted to do was slip back into oblivion, but the pills and alcohol had fried out of her system hours ago and the red glow she was seeing beyond her clenched eyelids meant a sunny day was well underway, or the apartment was on fire. Before Anna could open her eyes to find out which was the case, the harsh murmuring from the next room amped up to shouting, swearing, and the sound of breaking furniture.

She rolled over in bed, pounded on the wall with both bare feet and heard china breaking in the kitchen sink of the apartment on the other side of the thin wall. She hoped Gabe was home and that her front door was unlocked.

In less than a minute, Gabriel opened the bedroom door to find her with the pillow clamped over her head, one arm gesturing towards the living room where the sounds of mayhem and destruction escalated.

Gabriel was an imposing guy and when he was fired up, people tended to pay attention to his instructions. The yelling cut off. Now all she could hear was muffled voices, footfalls, a door slamming and then, blessed silence. Someone was pulling the pillow from her grasp. It was Gabriel, her savior, six-foot-two of muscle and menace topped off with a bad buzz-cut that natural blonds should avoid.

"Who the fuck were they?" he asked.

"I have no idea. I guess they brought Ray home from the bar last night."

"They broke the coffee table. Where is he?"

"Don't know. I'll be so glad when he gets his license back." It wasn't lost on either of them that Ray drove when he wanted to, despite not having a valid license. She tried to pull the pillow back over her face, but he held it out of reach.

"You?" he said, "I gotta ride to work with him until then. Can't afford to have him get busted. And you owe me two coffee mugs."

"I'm sorry. I was scared."

"And hungover." He didn't need to add 'again'.

"Thanks for coming over."

He crossed the hall to the bathroom and came back with a glass of water and three aspirins. Shaking his head, he said, "This shit's getting old."

"Yeah, it is."

He gave her back the pillow and she tucked it under her head. New pounding came from the other side of the wall. Gabriel closed his eyes. "I gotta go resume the daily reaming."

Anna groaned, "I hope this won't make things worse."

"Not possible." He patted her leg and grimaced. "Her mother sent her home with the latest issue of *Bride* magazine yesterday and somehow it got tossed in the trash with the spaghetti leftovers. I'll see you later." He pulled the sheet off her as he walked away. "Jesus Anna, the least you could do is sleep naked."

She smiled wanly and fell back on the pillow. Tears slipped down the side of her face and filled one of her ears, blocking all sounds except her own heartbeat.

THE FRONT DOOR BANGED OPEN, and she was jarred awake a second time. It was Ray in one of his frenzies making sure everyone else was up to his speed, or whatever he was doing at the moment. The pattern of his racket so familiar she could almost ignore it and go back to sleep, but she knew he'd soon be kicking the mattress under her. TV too loud, refrigerator door slammed. Silverware drawer yanked open, slammed shut. Twice. Toilet used and flushed; the bathroom door left open wide. He walked like he was wearing high heels. The mattress shuddered under her.

"Hey. Get the fuck up. It's nearly noon. You need to get your shit together. We're meeting a guy later and I need you to look tasty. He's a real gash hound so take some pains, could ya?" He started yanking hangers back and forth in the closet. "Is that blue dress clean? Are you listening to me?"

"After coffee, Ray." There was no point in asking for mercy.

THE GLASS PERCOLATOR seemed to take a long, slow forever on mornings like this, but she liked defying the 'watched pot never boils' adage by standing right in front of the stove and daring the brown gold to rain down from the glass and aluminum basket. Weak and aching to her bones, she felt like an old vampire waiting for a transfusion. She closed her eyes to rewind the events from the night before. Everything that had gotten her to this broken now.

Bobby was right, the tens were heavy. The joint on the ride home and the half bottle of Chardonnay when she got there had been a mistake. She smelled her hair and cringed, wondering how she could have gone to bed without showering.

Ray slammed another door and the noise and shift in air pressure led her to a replay of the night before; the dank and darkness of the garage when the fans kicked on, the adrenaline overload hiding from the danger, and that unsettling sexual rush she'd had when she was hiding. *What was that?*

This morning it didn't matter that there was no cream or milk. She took her cup and sat gingerly at the kitchen table. Bitter and black was the ticket.

Rather than clear the table, Ray had shoved dirty dishes to one side and left a series of documents out, one sheet of paper carefully overlapping the next, fanned out so whoever was looking could get the gist of the whole without having to touch the parts.

He can't do this! She shuffled through the papers, a deed, tax records, a survey. Hands shaking, she unfolded the plat that showed the land Ray had purchased. There, in the center of the property the deed described, was her aunt and uncle's small farm. Her home. The odd-shaped piece of land that surrounded it on three sides had been for sale for many years. No one could be bothered with it, least of all Murph.

"You can't do this," she said, loud and angry.

Ray looked at her incredulously. "As you can see by those papers," he snatched the map out of her hands, "which are none of your business, by the way, it's a done deal."

She wouldn't give him the satisfaction of asking what his plans for the property were. She already knew. He would develop it, put up any kind of shit he could get away with, effectively cutting off the farm's access to the dirt and gravel road that ran the length of the property. Owning the land surrounding the farm was as good as putting up an electric fence that she wouldn't dare cross.

Anna clutched the mug with both hands, her shoulders hunched. Ray loomed over her as he slowly gathered up the documents, holding each one under her nose before slipping it into a manila folder.

"You keep fucking with me and your ass'll be in prison. I'll send you pictures of them getting evicted and me driving a bulldozer over that shack. How d'you like that? Are we clear here?"

Anna didn't answer. He slammed his fist on the table and a wine glass fell off and shattered, spraying shards over her bare feet.

"Crystal," she whispered.

SAM SLUMPED on the window ledge behind her, seething with unspendable rage, a flexing shadow in the curtains. Her anger and fear simultaneously compelled him and kept him in check, but there were limits neither knew. Ray's threats, his naked disdain for her, made Sam grind his teeth and growl with frustration like a tiger on a short chain. A second glass shattered in sympathy.

~O~

An hour later Gabriel pulled the truck into the lumberyard. The parking lot was empty for a Saturday morning. It was a sign of the times, and he knew he was lucky to have a project that would carry him a couple more months. Inside the dim front office, a stretched-out telephone cord hung over the side of the counter, the receiver on the dirty tile floor. He lifted it up by the cord, put it back on the cradle, and the phone rang instantly. He picked it up and answered, "Cole's Lumber". No response. "Hello, Cole's." Nothing. He frowned and hung it back up. It rang again immediately; this time he let it ring.

Bill Cole stepped out of his office in the back, picked up the receiver and threw it to the floor. "Which is why the motherfucker was off the hook. The guy was supposed to be here yesterday to fix it."

"I hope they haven't been able to hear you," Gabriel said, looking down at the phone.

"Fuck em!" Bill shouted in the direction of the receiver. He put his hands on the counter, grinned, and said, "What can I do you out of Gabe?"

"I need to set up a delivery for Monday. Cheverini's ticket."

Bill turned and pulled a clipboard from the rack. "Tell him I said after this delivery he's got ten days to settle up. The cheap prick. I hope he doesn't pay *you* when he feels like it." Bill chewed the pencil and frowned, "Oh yeah. There was a guy here looking for you earlier. Friend of Gordy's looking for work."

Gabriel thought about the schedule for the days ahead. There was a lot of two-man stuff, heavy lifting, but Gordy couldn't cut it physically and he couldn't count on Ray to be there. Lately, Ray was more aggravating than useful on the site.

"Did he leave a number?"

"Nah, but he said he'd be outside in a white Cadillac. He looks like he could handle the work. Young guy."

"I didn't see a Caddy when I pulled in. If he comes back, get a number."

Hands on his hips, Bill said, "Do I look like your fucking Kelly Girl?"

GABRIEL STEPPED BACK out into the glare of the dusty parking lot and looked around. No Caddy. He walked to the end of the building and looked down the alley. There it was, a white Cadillac convertible, top down, parked in the shade. A guy was sitting in the back, his tan, well-muscled arms spread out across the seatback, his head tipped back. At first, Gabe thought he was sleeping. But then, over the guy's shoulder, he could see a girl's dark hair and the back of her bright pink blouse. Dude was getting his knob polished right there in the alley. Gabriel frowned. If he wasn't getting any, nobody was. He walked up quietly, cleared his throat, and aimed a soft kick at the chrome bumper.

"Scuse me."

The girl popped up like a prairie dog, her round mouth red, black eye makeup a mess. She looked like a plastic blowup doll he'd seen at a party once and Gabe started to laugh. A split second later, another girl who matched the first one right down to the smeared eye makeup, popped up in the front seat. This one had apparently been sleeping but now she reached over the seat and grabbed the other one by the hair and the two of them started screeching at each other in a foreign language.

The guy turned around. "Thanks. Great timing. She was almost getting the hang of it."

Gabe replied, "Well, fuck you very much, my man. Bill said you were looking for work, but it looks like you found something so, later." He turned and headed for his truck laughing to himself. He was about to open the truck door when the guy came galloping up behind him raising a cloud of dust.

"Dude, I'm sorry. You're Gordy's friend, Gabriel, right? I'm really sorry. I been here since seven and the girls were getting bored and wanted to leave. I had to entertain them. Name's Jack."

"Tough life, Jack." Gabriel looked him up and down. He looked seventeen, maybe eighteen, wild, longish hair, scruffy beard, just shy of six-foot, but fit, like he'd done a day's hard work recently. Gabriel felt old at twenty-five and envied the kid's place in the scheme of things—at 'go' with his options wide open.

"You got tools?"

"The basics."

"You done any framing?"

"Yeah," Jack lied.

"OK, Monday. Here at 6:30. Sober." Gabe paused. "Alone."

Gabriel looked over Jack's shoulder towards the convertible. The two girls were both in the back seat now, looking his way like a pair of goofy collies. He turned back to Jack and said, "Dude. Both of them?"

"They're twins, man. What are ya gonna do?" Jack said. "I'll see you Monday."

They didn't shake hands or exchange last names. That would come on Monday if the day panned out well for all parties.

~O~

S1:E29

Angels Rest had been stolen from its birthplace in northern Italy sometime around the turn of the century. The deed to the manor and the surrounding lands had been passed down father to son until a wastrel lost it in a card game on a transatlantic steamship crossing. The last son of the family line was a gambler, a losing gambler. He had never even seen the place and was unmoved at the signing of the papers.

Over the course of a year, the grand house was gutted and dismantled, the rocks numbered and crated. Crates were taken by oxcarts to a freight depot, then by rail to a shipyard and loaded into the hold of a steamship. After clearing the port of New York, the crates were sent by rail three hours north of the city on one of the dairy lines, then trucked to the mountaintop. Here they were spread out in a great field by laborers and inventoried by the architect's assistant clucking over his clipboard.

Immigrants from Italy worked the reconstruction. Men known for their skills with the stone lived with their families in barracks on farms near the site. They built the walls that marked the borders of the property and the cobbled stone roadbed that wound up the grade to the building site with native granite.

It was the highest point for miles around, overlooking the river and the rail line to the west and the post road in the valley to the east. The castle's foundation was also built from the dense local stone which was everywhere just under the surface of the soil. The fields gave birth to rocks every spring. No one could farm this part of New York without first becoming a stonemason.

Once the foundation was complete, the numbered stones were uncrated and the puzzle that would be reborn as Angels Rest took shape. Old-growth timber from the wilds of the state was cut and milled to order. Marble tile and stained-glass windows commissioned. The massive beams and roof trusses raised by teams of men and oxen.

It was dangerous work. There were grave injuries and inevitable deaths. Across the face of a huge section of oak destined to become the lintel over the main door, an anonymous craftsman carved the words "Angeli in pace" to honor those who had died. But, in fear of reprimand from the architect, the beam was installed with the sentiment facing down instead of out. Even before the building was completed, Angels Rest was a birthplace for unsettled, unhappy spirits and no one who lived in the castle ever prospered.

New owners redecorated, gardens were torn up and replanted, or ignored and allowed to run wild. Lavish lifestyles and grand parties inevitably led to scandals, divorces, bankruptcies, and suicides. There were many disappearances and unsolved murders. In time, Angels Rest became a hotel on the post road, a stop along the way to points north. Rest awhile, then move along. Unsavory doings were the order of the day. No one bothered with rumors.

By 1910, many of the farms and hamlets up and down the river had been wiped out as the New York City reservoir system dammed the river to hold drinking water for the city. This part of the country reeked of history. There were more ghosts than living people. At the foot of the same property, there was a clapboard farmhouse built in 1790. It had a giant Dutch-style dairy barn that had allegedly been a stop on the Underground Railroad that had been set on fire to flush out people hiding there. Somewhere in dusty library stacks of old county newspapers some or all of these things could be documented but no one had yet taken the trouble to look.

The manor changed hands every decade or so, each new owner succumbing to the bad luck and poor judgment that seemed to come with every closing. In the late sixties, an aspiring slumlord purchased the building for back taxes and bribes and hastily divided it into a handful of poorly laid out apartments. Again, Angels Rest changed hands for the worse. Somewhere a building inspector was getting rich overlooking code violations. Tenants rented month by month. They came and went as plumbing leaks and electrical problems went unrepaired. The house was plagued with unhappiness and failures of circumstance and character.

On the ground floor were the remains of what had once been a grand ballroom complete with black and white marble floors and floor-to-ceiling windows that were overgrown with ivy on the outside. This is where the party started on Fridays, but people drifted in and out of any open door in the best and worst traditions of a sixties-style commune. By dark, the air was blue with marijuana and the dented trash cans lined up in the lobby were overflowing with beer cans and liquor bottles.

The closest town was Dean's Bridge. Only two hours by train from Manhattan, it was a typical small town that was dying slowly because it had no access to the interstate that bisected it. Everyone knew everyone's business and if your name was known in more than four towns spread over two counties, you were *either notorious, wanted by the cops for questioning, or running for political office.*

Every little town or four corners had its own Angels Rest. The unofficial place where it all went down.

~O~

When Anna snatched the note off the front door, the tape took a rectangle of brown paint with it, exposing a layer of filthy beige underneath. She tore the note up without reading it. The phone rang inside, but she was in no hurry to answer since it was probably Ray. He only left notes when he was expecting a command performance.

In the dim, dispirited bedroom, she dropped her folio in the corner and sat heavily on the end of the double bed. Something swaddled in plastic was draped over the standing mirror with another taped-on note. In Ray's cramped backhand, 'Be ready at 8'.

"Fuck that shit!" She ripped the plastic bag off the dress —a floor-length black thing—the strapless, satin bodice covered with dangling red sequins. It looked like a case of smallpox. The dress was obviously too small. It was bad enough when Ray hounded her weeks in advance, but this last-minute insult was the limit. The phone rang again, and she pounced on it ready to spit in his face, but it wasn't Ray.

Gina said, "Girl, if I don't go out tonight, I'm gonna go nuts. You busy?"

Without waiting for an explanation, Anna replied, "Be here in an hour. I have to get out of here myself or I'm gonna kill him."

Driving around in Gina's MG with the top down was all they had in common when they were high school seniors, both restless and bored. Gina had been looking for a husband. 'Rich' was her first prerequisite followed closely by 'hot'. Anna was looking for a little uncomplicated fun before going away to college. Ray had been a placeholder even then.

Early on, Anna read Gina in a perfunctory way and found her to be exactly as she presented herself—driven to succeed at something, but not wanting to work too hard at it. Gina was painfully honest but loyal to those who returned the same. Teen-aged girls couldn't ask for much more from their friends. Anna never let Gina know about her ability. She'd learned that hard lesson with Ray and never made the mistake again.

Gina had a sense of lawless adventure that got them into situations that Anna would never have considered by herself. They cruised all the blacktop and concrete between the Hudson River and the Atlantic—Connecticut, Rhode Island, even Massachusetts. Every now and then, they'd get into a little pace and chase with a guy in another sports car which sometimes ended with a stoplight exchange of phone numbers hastily jotted on a hand or scrap of paper.

Last fall, Gina was driving too fast for the wet roads and spun out, leaving the rear end of her car in a ditch. A highway department truck was first on the scene and the foreman, Ted, got his crew to pull the tiny car out and of course, got Gina's phone number. Ted met only one of her husband criteria, nonetheless, they dated and were sharing an apartment within weeks and Gina and Anna's adventures on wheels tapered off to almost nothing. It had been months since they'd gone bar hopping and Anna suspected trouble in Paradise.

Anna threw the dress back over the mirror where Ray couldn't miss it. On the other side of his note, she wrote 'get a hooker' and stuck it to the dress with the same piece of tape. She showered and changed quickly and was waiting outside when the shiny red car pulled up.

Ted had given Gina crap about going out—as if he had a right to tell her what she could or couldn't do—and Gina was in a pissy mood. Anna suspected that her friend was just bored with the whole domestic goddess thing and wanted out.

As different as their situations were, Anna felt her own rut closing in around her. She needed some fun—music and dancing! She would drink and get high to protect herself against the barrage of other people's emotional garbage. Then she'd be ready for whatever happened, and perfectly willing to make a spectacle of herself, Anna rarely remembered the best nights out and never had any regrets.

THE BAND PLAYING the Stateline was supposed to be good, so they made it their first stop. The parking lot was packed, but Gina wedged her car between two awkwardly parked, over-sized pickup trucks on the notion they wouldn't be staying.

They sat in the car and, while Gina filled her in on the latest, Anna smoked a whole joint almost by herself. The big news was that Gina had finalized her decision to dump Ted and was planning on getting into real estate. She was on the prowl, but not shopping for a new boyfriend.

"At this place? Please," Gina checked her makeup and retouched her already perfect lipstick. Then, as she did every time they got together, she asked, "When are you going to dump that bastard?"

Anna usually replied, "It's complicated." Tonight, however, she put up her hand and said nothing. She didn't even want to think about it.

THE BAR GOT a ton of traffic from Connecticut where the drinking age was still twenty-one. If young stuff was your game, male or female, the Stateline was the place to go. The bouncer was new, and Anna was simultaneously flattered and wistful as they were carded at the door. She would turn twenty-six in the fall. Life was passing her by, and she hadn't even waved at it. Her relationship with Ray was deadlocked. He would never let her go and she couldn't run away. She was down to one option, but so far, it was only a fantasy.

The Yard Dogs were just about to break out and make it big. Rumor had it that a record deal was in the works and that they'd be touring nationally before September. The band got as much appreciation for their original music as they did for great covers. They even had a couple of horn players. It was good music for a sweaty workout after a couple of drinks—with a guy if you were lucky, one of your girlfriends if you weren't.

The place was filling up quickly and the girls nabbed two empty stools at the end of the bar closest to the dance floor. Anna slipped her sandals off and tucked them under the bar rail. Gina looked at her friend's bare feet and grimaced. "I don't know how you can stand it."

Anna replied, "In ten minutes, I won't care. Right, Sal?"

The bartender said, "That's right, honey. Alcohol is a great antiseptic."

Determined to wall herself off from everyone's mental scatter, Anna downed two tequila sunrises in quick succession. Gina was as cheap as Ray and ordered a draft beer that she would nurse until it was flat while she passed judgment on everyone in the room.

They had a routine–Anna drank as much as she wanted in the first hour, then stopped and let Gina catch up if they decided to stay. By closing time, one of them was usually sober enough to get them home in one piece.

Anna dug into her purse for some cash and found a travel-worn pill at the bottom. She frowned at it a moment trying to figure out what it was. Greenish and fuzzy. She shrugged and swallowed it, then held her empty glass up to the bartender and winked at him. The music was already going straight to her bones and muscles, and she was aching to move.

THAT AFTERNOON, the band had arrived at the Newburgh airport from Detroit. At the last minute, they needed another car. Stuck for a driver, Gordy reluctantly pressed Jack into service.

"Dude, just follow me and keep it between the lines, okay?"

Jack agreed to drive because the limo would transport the guitars and luggage only—no humans. There was no way he could stay cooped up with a squad of drug-tattered, ego-tripping rock stars for two hours.

Everyone arrived at the Stateline in one piece. They ditched the band and were doing a brisk business; Gordy was a trusted source for all manner of pills, while Jack brought a welcome level of quality weed. Tonight, Jack was offering something powerful, allegedly from Hawaii.

A trio of girls and two guys joined them at a table. Jack had smoked pot in the parking lot, done shots of bourbon at the bar, and drunk his share of bottomless pitchers of beer at the table. One of the girls produced what she thought was a 'lude. No one could be sure in the light. She crushed it, mixed it into her cocktail and split it with him, Jack taking the crunchy dregs. Before long, he was loudly holding forth on ballroom dancing.

"Look, all I'm saying is when you dance with a chick like this, you already have your hands on her. Am I right, ladies?" Jack felt a flash of pity for those who had never learned the art of dancing in another's arms.

TWO OF THE girls were looking at him fixedly, mouths slightly open. He was an annoying paradox. Maureen already knew Jack. Biblically. She was pretty sure he didn't remember pulling her into a stall in the ladies' room the last time Gordy had brought him around. Then Jack winked at her as he drained a mug of draft, convincing her otherwise. Some guys were only good for one thing and Jack was very good at it, but she was here with a new boyfriend—one with a full-time job and a new car. Still, Jack had her rapt attention.

"So, you already got her pretty little hand in yours and your other hand," Jack waggled his fingers in the air, "is on her ass. A few tight spins around the floor and you're a boner away from closing the deal. If you can't make that pay off, you got bigger problems then I can help you with."

Earlier, he'd tried to get one of the girls out on the floor to a rock song so he could show off, work the ballroom thing, but she'd flatly refused. She'd seen Jack dance once and wasn't high enough to want to look like an idiot.

One of the guys, confident that he was suave in his polyester jumpsuit said, "I had enough trouble picking up on this disco shit. I'll be damned if I'll take dancing lessons to get laid. Looks gay to me."

Jack leaned across the table and beckoned him close with one hand, then smacked him, friendly-like, on the side of his head and said, "Listen to yourself, fool. All I know is I been getting my share, and most of yours since I learned the fucking box step." He plucked a cherry from one of the girl's drinks and popped it in his mouth. "They don't call it that for nothing, you know."

Without really knowing why, the girls all giggled.

Jack leaned back in his chair and closed his eyes to gauge the level of his high. Stable, but definitely well-baked —right where he liked to be at this point in the evening. Anything could still happen. He could hear the music at a cottony remove and the floor was still firm under his feet. If he got up, would he walk or fly? The air around his face stirred and he felt a chill. The noise in the room receded further, and from somewhere inside his head, a sexy woman's voice whispered, *Look at her!*

He opened his eyes, and she was all he could see. Her sun-striped hair was gathered with a scrap of blue cloth into a thick ponytail that tumbled down her back drawing his gaze to an ample ass. Barefooted and tan, she had one leg curled languidly around the leg of the stool, toes pointed like a ballerina, her posture regal. She lifted her chin to an angle of challenge, held her glass high, and said something to the bartender giving Jack a glimpse of full lips curving into a wicked smile.

He stared at her as conversation and laughter swirled

around him, then realized he was moving his head whenever his line of sight to her was blocked by people coming
and going. That voice inside his head again, a warm whisper. *Go on now. Go get her!*

Without a word to anyone, Jack got up, waded across the
crowded dance floor, and stood behind her staring at the
place where her neck curved into her shoulder, wondering
what she would taste like there. Wondering what he was
doing.

Anna was having an animated argument with the
bartender about the toxicity of maraschino cherries. "Sal,
come on. You'd have to eat a whole jar three times a day to
even get indigestion. Make me another one."

Sal stood in front of her patiently, noting her slur. He
poked Gina in the back with his finger. "Are you driving?"

Gina wasn't having a good time. Several guys had asked
her to dance but she had dismissed them all. She held out a
cigarette for Sal to light and said sourly, "Starting to look
that way."

Sal took her glass and Anna slapped the bar top. "My
man! If I ever blame anything I do on being loaded, you
have permission to hurt me." She swung her foot in time
with the music and drank deeply. The tequila and whatever
that pill was, rolled together and amped up the weed, all of
it giving her a thick, cushiony buzz. The cherries exploded
in her mouth when she bit down on them and the ice in her
glass gave off sparks. The smells and flavors of the room, the
people, were vivid, complex, and compelling. The only
emotions and thoughts Anna was having were her own. Her
glide was on.

She was feeling gloriously omniscient when someone
salty and vibrant cupped a large, warm hand around her
elbow and said, "Hey, let's go". He had a deep, resonant voice

and didn't seem to have a clue about rejection. She turned in her seat, but his head and broad, bare shoulders eclipsed the bright lights of the stage, his face in full shadow. The glitter of a gold earring sparkled from unkempt hair. None of that mattered—between his voice and the gentle, insistent touch, a thrill went through her like current.

Without waiting for an answer, he shifted his hand from her arm to her waist, boosted her off the stool, and aimed her toward the dance floor. Anna grinned over her shoulder at Gina with mock alarm. Gina raised her beer and gave her a pitying look.

Eagerly, she wove her fingers through his and towed the mystery man a half step behind her. The band dropped the downbeat of a raucous, drum-heavy cover of "Can't Get Enough of Your Love", but Jack didn't back away from her. Instead, he pulled her close, planted his hand on the curve of her hip and began to drive her through a loose rumba that he tailored expertly to the bouncing beat.

Anna was a decent dancer, and she was thrilled to be led, for once, by someone better. *Nobody dances like this anymore!*

People began to watch, making space for them on the scuffed floor—a bearded longhair, shirtless in faded overalls and high-top sneakers and a busty, barefooted woman in a short summer dress moving gracefully around the floor in an old-fashioned dance. By the time the song was over, they were almost alone, dancing as if they had learned the steps together years ago.

From the cloud she was riding, Anna accepted that somehow, he was inside her head, making it possible for him to anticipate her every move. Or was it the other way around? She felt her will being replaced by her partner's desire. His strong arms were bright with sweat that soaked into her senses like sweet oil. There was a white, wolfish smile somewhere in that scruffy beard. Through all the contact, she sensed wood, steel, concrete, and blood. A taste that made her hungry. *Is this what I've waited for? To be bossed around by a tender confidence. Tuned and played by someone until I come apart at the seams and evaporate. It doesn't matter who he is or isn't. He's real, I can feel it.*

The song ended and the crowd cheered for them and the band. Jack took a theatrical bow and Anna tried to curtsy but lost her footing and stumbled. He caught her before her ass hit the floor making it look like one more smooth move.

The band took a break, but within seconds, "Into the Mystic" bloomed from the jukebox. Like a preacher, the insistent opening beats commanded all the lovers in the room to rise and join. Jack pulled Anna close. She shook her head. *I don't know how.* A lie. She'd learned it years ago.

"It's only a heartbeat. Feel it." He counted off, his beard tickling her ear as they moved around the floor again, this time, a tango. Not the flashy, macho tango people knew from the movies and not the formal, traditional dance with all its aggressive posturing and frills. Jack's tango was a dance of quiet possession. Banked passion. He found the beat he needed in the bass line of the unlikely ballad, made the moves, and took her with him, and, to his delight, she flowed with him like a river, unerringly nailing the syncopated beats.

Bodies touching, full turns cut to a quarter, moves held beats longer than the rhythm asked. Abandoning any pretense of form, Jack pulled her hand to his heart with one hand and cupped her ass with the other. He meant to have her.

He tried to see her face, her eyes, but she ducked her

head to his shoulder and drew her long fingernails gently over his exposed nipple. He almost staggered with the throb cycling between his heart and his cock. *If she moves like this in bed, I'm a dead man.*

The music was muffled by the sound of his own blood rushing through his head. He was hot and cold at the same time. He wished desperately that he'd passed on those last shots of bourbon, feeling it all like a deep acid flashback. The tastes of honey and butter fought in his mouth as the music carried them deeper into uncharted waters.

Like the Petty girls on the vintage calendars hanging on the walls of Murph's shop, she was all legs, tits and ass. Her flesh was overpowering his senses and she wasn't even working at it. She smelled like oranges and Christmas and moved like she had no bones. He tried to read her and couldn't and it was maddening. She was right there in his arms and yet she wasn't.

Jack tugged on one end of her scarf to watch her hair cascade around her shoulders. People still watching gave a smattering of applause, and he leaned back to see her reaction. Her eyes were closed, that deadly smile hinting that she was in command and loving every minute of it. *That mouth!* He curled his arm around her shoulder, spun her away and reeled her back in, fitting his mouth over hers, his arms around her tight.

As the song ended, she held the kiss, boldly drifting her tongue across his bottom lip, then sucking on it gently. The crowd's whistling and applause broke the spell and she retreated, turning her head but breathing one word into his ear, or was it his soul? *More.*

The club owner picked up the microphone. "Hey, hey, hey, people! Who knew your cover included a floor show, right? Let's hear it for..." he leaned out to them, cupping his hand to his ear, then shouted, "Hannah and her yak!" to applause, whistles, and catcalls from the crowd.

The band's leader took the microphone from the manager, waved his arms at the crowd and said, "Yeah, yeah, we know what you want. More of the same, right?" and the band launched into a tight cover of "Rock Me, Baby". Before she could get away, Jack gathered Anna into his arms again and danced her through the crowd and out the side door to the parking lot.

THE DRUGS, alcohol, and the emotional whirlwind had her nearly senseless, but she knew she couldn't walk across the rocky lot barefooted. "My feet are somewhere. I..." There was something more she needed to say to him, but the words were out of reach.

Without asking, Jack picked her up, slung her over his shoulder, and carried her out to the trio of limos parked in the darkness. He put her down and they stood by the open car door, lit up by the interior light. He kissed her again holding her face with both hands, a power kiss this time. Forgetting how to breathe, his every intention on the line with lips, tongue, and teeth.

She leaned into him, holding on to the straps of his over-alls, kissing him back, welcoming him in, every nip and suckle signaling her desire for more as he sank down to the seat, pulling her onto his lap. Both glowing with lust, the physical passion was suddenly overshadowed by an ominous energy that flickered between them from danger to wonder and back again and they both felt it. Someone was going to get burned but neither of them cared.

Jack pulled his mouth away from hers and whispered, "Woman, what's your story?"

Before she could think of a reply, someone was shouting from a few paces away. It was Gina, furiously sober.

"There you are!" Gina grabbed Anna by the arm and pulled her to her feet. "Sorry, Farmer Fred," Gina looked Jack up and down with disdain as he got out to stay close to Anna. "Nice moves, but her old man will be giving me a big bag of shit if I don't bring her home and I am leaving in three minutes. Make your bye-byes."

Old man? Jack felt his heart skid and contract. *Was she married?*

"These juveniles from Connecticut have ruined this place for me!" Gina dropped Anna's purse and sandals in the dirt, turned on her heel, and headed to the idling sports car.

Anna sank to the door sill of the limo and started to struggle into her sandals. Jack knelt and put them on for her, his sweaty forehead on her knees, breathing in her heat. She closed her eyes and rested her head on his while he lingered over the task. He kissed her knees and helped her stand. "When can I see you again?"

She was unsteady on her feet, and he wrapped his arms around her from behind as she wrote a phone number in the dirt on the roof of the car with one slow finger.

Not if, but when! He buried his face in her hair, but they both were yanked back from oblivion by the racket of a car crunching the gravel right beside them, horn bleating. He helped her into the tiny car and closed the door gently at a loss for what else he could do or say.

Anna leaned her head on the window and watched him until she couldn't see him anymore. *Why is this so out of control? What's happened to me?*

. . .

THE SPORTS CAR churned up dust and turned south. Jack watched it disappear into the dark. He tried to think back over the last fifteen or twenty minutes. *A couple of dances and a stroll across the parking lot?* The only thing she had said to him was something about her feet and he couldn't hear her when she told the MC her name. *Hannah?* He didn't think the man had heard either of them.

He took a pen from a clipboard on the front seat and copied the number on his forearm and, for good measure, the thigh of his overalls. He wandered back into the club dazed, still wondering when he'd been bewitched. The first moment he saw her? That hair and her ass? Her bare foot keeping time to the music? But deep down, he knew there was more than what could be seen. He'd never had a partner get it so effortlessly right. She was there in his arms as flesh and blood as a woman could be, and yet, she wasn't.

Gord was waiting for him at the bar. He'd quickly claimed Anna's seat when Jack had taken her onto the dance floor. He'd tried to strike up a conversation with Gina, but the dark-haired beauty had looked at him like he was rancid and turned her back on him. He'd been left with the queen of snotty bitches.

"What the fuck was that all about, dude?" Gord shouted, laughing and clapping Jack on the shoulder. "I thought we were gonna keep a low profile tonight and do a little more business, but noooo! Jack gets dazzled by blond boobies and we get the Fred and Ginger show. And anyway, when the fuck did you learn to dance like my mother?" He dug Jack in the ribs with his elbow, spilling his beer. "Bartender!" Gord shouted, "Bring this man some grog! His buzz is wearing thin!"

Jack was suddenly sober with the hollowness that comes after burning off a serious bender with a long, hard sleep.

He scrubbed his hands over his face and blinked at his reflection in the dirty mirror behind the bar. He could still smell her. His groin ached. To no one in particular, he said, "I think I'm in love."

Gord made a face and punched him in the arm. "Snap out of it, fool."

What Jack couldn't stop wondering was why?

~O~

(CONTINUED in *Prophets Tango ~ Season 2: Dancing in the Dark*)

THANK YOU

Thank you for falling into *Prophets Tango*. I had such a great time writing it. Do you really think I could stop here?

If you're enjoying *Prophets Tango*, please leave a review wherever you purchased it, then go to https://www.lacativa.com/ and sign up to be notified when the next book becomes available. Leave a message. I'd love to hear from you. You can find me here too: https://linktr.ee/deblacativa.

www.ingramcontent.com/pod-product-compliance
Lightning Source LLC
Chambersburg PA
CBHW022200170626
46807CB00005B/2283